HISTORIES

HISTORIES

Sam Guglani

riverrun

First published in Great Britain in 2017 by

riverrun

An imprint of

Quercus Editions Limited
Carmelite House
50 Victoria Embankment
London EC4Y 0DZ

An Hachette UK company

Lines from *Four Quartets* by T. S. Eliot, published by Faber and Faber Ltd,
reprinted with permission from Faber and Faber Ltd.
Lines from *Dream Song 207* by John Berryman, published by Faber and Faber Ltd.
Lines from *A Sudden Meeting* by Rabindranath Tagore, translated by Pratima Bowes,
published by East West publications.
Any omissions should be notified to the publishers, who will be pleased to make restitution.

A CIP catalogue record for this book is available
from the British Library.

Hardback 978 1 78648 380 5
Trade Paperback 978 1 78648 382 9
Ebook 978 1 78648 383 6

10 9 8 7 6 5 4 3 2 1

Typeset by CC Book Production
Printed and bound in Great Britain by Clays Ltd, St Ives plc

HISTORIES

Dev Bhatia, consultant physician

Monday, 24 October

I T REMINDS HIM OF school, the sun coming in like this, low through windows, lighting the corridor. This time of year especially. He thinks of new terms and stiff collars, the smell of school dinners and swimming pools. A feeling of arrival and separation, still, after all these years.

Dev navigates the maze: cleaners' wet-floor placards, parked trolleys shedding pillows and blankets, debris left out from the mad night's retreating tide. He feels it in the mornings, in the silence, like a storm has passed.

Voices, then bodies, surface and drift towards him. An early morning round, moving like a hunting pack from ward to ward. He exchanges nods with Nathan Munro – pale, giant, crisp-suited archetype of a consultant – speaking into a Dictaphone as he lopes unflinchingly forward in polished shoes. A nurse and some juniors follow, tugged like gulls in the wake of a fishing boat. As they pass, fragments of Nathan's dictation fall away: *this unfortunate . . . disease . . . sadly . . . survival.* Hospital words spun like stones across the still waters of people's lives. The juniors follow on, shuffling their lists, stumbling and trying to keep up, to mimic their consultant's easy movement.

Dev hears one of them say, Beached whale, wasn't she? He stops, stares, prepares to admonish, but his phone hums with Peter's text: *On way. S worried. Tx.* When he looks up again, Nathan and the entourage have walked away.

It's early in Outpatients, the waiting room still empty, only a student sitting reading. Dev recognises her from his rounds, remembers she's keen and notices things, recalls her unusual seriousness. Her hair falls in a plait over one shoulder, almost touching the pages of her book. And he remembers that little girl in India, from when he was a student himself.

He'd no stethoscope that day, and he'd listened to the tight wheeze with his ear pressed to her back, staring out at her frightened mother in the heavy light. He'd raced back to the jeep and returned with bronchodilators, waiting and watching as the girl settled. She was beautiful, sick, unlucky. Even then he wondered at these separate lines, how they converge indifferently, blindly, in everyone. Maybe it was that encounter, persisting and blossoming, that brought him to respiratory medicine, to the troubled breath of so many.

The receptionist and nurse prepare his clinic, busily checking through notes and lists. Morning, Dr Bhatia. Morning, Dr Bhatia. *Bat-yer*. Like Dev was briefly Dave when he started here. Like they'd all had a meeting and decided on it: *Let's bloody well call him Dave, shall we?*

That was a strange time, ten years ago, from East London to this other, surreal England. Now they're more cautious than curious, quietening as he arrives, unimpressed by his lack of frivolity, that trait so desired by doctors, so oddly necessary.

He calls over to the clinic nurse, Peter Nicholls and his wife will be here shortly, they're not booked in but I need a few minutes with them. I'll wait in my room, thanks very much. These last words delivered like a no-nonsense Englishman, like he's ordering a five-star breakfast. He hates how it veers into his voice, the camouflage of a doctor's tone. He recognises the nurse – she works on the wards usually – and he tries again. Thanks, Lucy, he says. She smiles at him, or rather at his closing door.

The clinic room is a continuation of the corridor's frenzy. He starts to tidy it, putting away others' files and notes, brushing down the desk. But then he looks around: a loose ceiling tile, a plastic glove on the floor, a redundant poster of the inner ear. Extraordinary when it's really seen, the messy truth of a hospital, so far removed from our pristine fantasies.

The window looks out onto Emergency, the staff car park, a steady train of people. Someone, one of the porters, whistles. A cloud passes and the light intensifies, squares of it falling on an outside wall, brightening the high twigs of a tree. Some years ago, early one morning, there'd been an eclipse. He hadn't gone out, but had looked on from this same window as patients and staff were drawn out of the building; as if, for a moment, they shared some quickened time, some actual sense of the world's brevity as the daylight diminished around them.

He signs off some letters. *Kind regards, yours sincerely, best wishes.* Decorative phrases, like wearing ties. When will we look back at letters like this, at ties, and just laugh? He keeps asking Hannah, his secretary, to delete the pointless formalities, but here they still are, kept and framed; enduring courtesies in lieu of actual patient care, like so much of the organisation. That's what hospitals are called now: *organisations.* He sighs, then smiles at his sighing.

He checks the time: ten more minutes. Opening a folder of results, he quickly flicks through them. Stops. Last week, one evening in his office, he'd become breathless and tearful on reading a patient's scan report: a young man's tumour relapsing, someone he's known for years, someone he likes very much. Hundreds of these results in cardboard folders or on screens, handfuls of them two or three times a week for years now. Part of the fabric of his day, like signing off scripts or checking e-mails. Then this sudden emotion – bizarre, unsettling.

Empathy seems to him such a narrow possibility, like close-hauling a dinghy into the wind. Just a degree or two either side and the sail loosens, flapping uselessly into senti-ment or self-regard. So these hot, new tears felt incontinent, like signs of trouble.

But he's always been disorientated by reading results, hasn't he? The act of opening them, of seeing someone's future laid out, whole days, sometimes whole weeks before they know of or experience it. Like reading fortunes. He said this once, in passing, to James Chester. Jim just chuckled absent-mindedly, a proper social laugh, turning away from Dev to pour coffee, flaunting his perfectly choreographed resilience. My patients are always complaining I don't have the results on time, he said. Not that I'm reading their bloody tarot cards.

But look at us, Dev wanted to say, look at how we accumulate losses.

Lucy's head appears at the door. They're here, she says, I told them you wouldn't be long. He thanks her, stands to wash his face, checks himself in the mirror, a hand through his hair.

They want his thoughts on some symptoms Sara's been having. Peter, as a radiologist, might easily have arranged a scan for her. That sort of thing still happens all the time: doctors sorting out their families and friends, despite the law and the frowns, still shortcutting the system.

Not that coming to see Dev is that much better. But what could he have said? He and Peter had been juniors together at Guy's, had stayed in contact and now, though not friends, were comfortable colleagues. Peter had settled in so easily after starting here, all forearms and checked shirts, a ready humour and a large private practice. Strange, really, that they hadn't asked for a private opinion. Hadn't Nathan looked after her in the first place? Nathan, the groomed ambassador of mighty medicine. Dev's flattered they've come to him instead, though mainly he wants to see her again.

He met her at their charity bash over the summer, and had been surprised at the sheer glitz of it. He's used to medicine's odd glamour, starting as it does in medical school almost regardless of one's background, the obligatory and regular spells of decadence and excess. He's never worked out what to make of it all, whether it's just some odd assertion of status, or a similarly odd push back against all the suffering that's met and denied.

Even so, the Nicholls' party had been quite something. Their friends, the cars, the dresses, the auction prizes and pledges. He half expected the fabled wife-swapping to declare itself, though of course he'd have been left with nothing to offer.

When he first started here, there'd been cursory efforts to try and fix him up. More, he felt, for the theatre of it than any genuine concern for his well-being, similar in impulse and execution to his mother's attempts at an arranged marriage for him, something he'd hoped to escape on leaving London.

But that all seemed another life, another him. He prefers being alone now, prefers the silence and the space. There have been occasional, brief relationships. Not that he isn't lonely, but the loneliness, he is sure, is less a function of being single and more one of being human.

But he'd been caught by her at the party. They'd found themselves sitting on the stairs, talking about his work and strangely, quickly about death. She told him about her cancer. Years ago, she said, such a small thing. And this annual party to somehow mark it, to support the research. She'd looked out over her glass at the guests, mused at how they hoped to inoculate themselves through charitable donations. Vaccinating against their own mortality, she said. Fur coats can do that, you know. She laughed, but something in how she said it – without contempt or gossip, understanding of the human folly – had made him stop and look at her.

He'd had a few drinks and found himself confiding in a way he hadn't since . . . when? He talked about waiting for the autumn, about how he loved it, how it seemed to surface in the full throes of summer, the light deepening and the leaves turning already. How it felt to him that life visibly contained the fact of death, just millimetres inside its translucent skin. She laughed, her head thrown back. He can still see it: the curve of her neck, the perfect white arc of it like a half moon, a single brown mark by her ear. She touched his face, easily, enormously. That's not death, she said. That *is* life, Dr B, you'd best get a good look at it. She laughed again then lowered her hand.

He hears laughter outside now and opens his door to see the two of them at the nurses' station, Peter leaning on the desk and teasing Lucy, Sara next to him. Ah, Peter says, looks like the good doctor will see us now.

Dev ushers them in. They shake hands and sit, preamble

a little – Peter's department gossip, holidays, how long it's been. A breath, then Sara starts. She talks about her pain, the weight loss, looking straight at him. We trust you, so we wanted your thoughts. Would you mind just checking? I know it sounds silly but would you mind?

Peter chips in: Mammograms, smears – all fine. She needs a CT, at least an ultrasound, he says. But, well, you know.

Dev offers to examine her briefly. Would that be OK? I'll draw the curtains round, in case someone charges in, he jokes. They laugh. He suggests Peter come in too if they prefer, but Peter raises a hand, says he'll wait in his chair, thanks very much, leave the proper doctoring to Dev.

He lowers the couch, asks her to lie down and lift her blouse a little. He washes his hands with his back to her. His heart feels loud in this small space, the lights too bright and Peter just outside the curtain, in this same room. She looks pale, drawn, beautiful. He comes to the trolley side. What did she say? Is she saying something to him? And Peter, just there, the nurses in the corridor, then the whole hospital and the people outside in the street.

His hand's contact with Sara's abdomen is deliberate, perfect, not like the other times – hundreds, surely – he has done this before without any thought. Four quadrants, light then deep palpation. The automatic tilting and balloting learnt by rote for exams, like times tables. He stops, almost calls in a nurse to chaperone. Why hasn't he? Of course he can't, not now, ridiculous now.

Let me know, he says, if it hurts at all. She nods, her eyes on him, like at the party, on the stairs. He sees her laughing, her head thrown back. But examining her, he's steadied again in the rhythm and escape of medicine. He talks her through it. Deep breath in. And out. Is that . . . Can he really feel a liver edge? Enlarged, pressed out like a child's angry lip? His face keeps it under a series of blinks. Everything so easily concealed.

He remembers removing his first tunnelled-line as a houseman. The young, frightened lad asking how many times he'd done it before. Oh, twenty or thirty, he said. Easy, you won't feel a thing. The lie so immediate and accessible, only weeks into his career. The lie of confidence and certainty, knowledge kept until it's ripe to fall. Her liver. Won't feel a thing. Breathe in. And out.

Just sit up please, thanks Sarah, almost done. You OK out there, Dr Nicholls? Peter returns a muffled, Yep. Standing behind her, her blouse loose, he sees the white of her bra, the drop of her back. He examines her neck, feels for nodes, doubting now what he's felt in her abdomen. Her soft, pale skin, and there, the mark by her ear. He leans in, kisses it. Soundless, real. The room swings, like his head's been thrown back, but no, nothing has moved. She stays still, stays sitting. He continues, percussing through her blouse, checking expansion, more breaths, his hands still on her. She says nothing. That's fine, he says, all done, you can get up now.

Before she can turn to him, he walks quickly to the sink, his back to her again. He hears the whisper of her clothes, the skirt zip, the curtains pulled back and the chair's creak as she sits with Peter.

He turns, tensing for what must surely come, his pulse racing, his body moving without thought. She lifts her eyes as he sits back with them. Nothing. Not a thing. They both wait for him. All of them wait.

Josh Webster, hospital porter

Saturday, 29 October

IT'S LIKE WE'RE INVISIBLE. They see us – God knows they bleep us enough – but it's like we're part of the building. Or like we're attachments to trolleys and wheel-chairs. The way things are going round here, we probably will be soon. Robots fixed to the ends of beds, whizzing around on wheels or jetpacks. I hope not. The doctors maybe, but not us, not in my time, please. It's not just about losing the work or money. Of course that'd be a struggle, Lucy and I buying a place and all. But then look around, who's not struggling? No, it's more the thought of being in that kind of hospital. All shine and surface. Nothing human to reach from or out to. Nothing real.

Lucy and I went to London last weekend and we saw this show. More a circus, really. Magic tricks and performers; big, old-fashioned songs. They had these life-sized puppets, like fairy-tale characters, held and moved about by men and women in black Lycra. They stood behind the puppets, working the arms and legs, doing all the talking, making the whole story happen. You could see them doing it, but after a while it was like you stopped seeing them.

I told the boys about it back at work, how it reminded me of what we did. They laughed but they weren't having it. They said they were sick of not being noticed or appreciated, of working as hard as anyone but not being recognised for it.

That's a big thing in here, in this hospital – maybe all hospitals. Everyone's so desperate to be noticed, to be acknowledged and clocked as important. The boys always announce themselves loudly when they arrive on the ward, thundering in and making a big show of it. I prefer to go unnoticed myself. The less you're seen, I think, or the less you try to be seen, the more you really do see.

This hospital's trying to find itself a new mission statement, a new grand vision to unite us all. So, here's my penny's worth: *IT'S NOT ABOUT US*. Put that up in the staff rooms. Or get switch to bleep us with it every hour. Paint it in big letters on the front of the hospital, if you like. Maybe even in Latin.

I helped out last week with the doctors' exams. The first time I did it I was surprised that they carry on with all this stuff, even after they're qualified – on and on, sometimes for years. It was the same drill as before: a load of patients gathered in the clinic area, me and the others bringing them in from the wards or meeting them at the entrance.

This would have terrified me once, all that sickness in one small space, the weight of it. But last week it felt like a bit of a party. Patients arriving like grand guests. I imagined myself announcing them. *Mrs Thingy of Wherever with Thyrotoxicosis.* I should have done it, too. I'll do it next year. Or one year, the very last year before I retire. The punters'd love it.

They get set up in the clinic rooms ahead of the doctors arriving in their smart clothes, looking nervous for once. If it really was a party, the docs would be like nerdy teenagers turning up too early and awkward in their glad rags. This nurse said to me once how it was like an old Victorian freak show, the patients, their pathologies, all laid out on display for the strolling medics. Maybe. But I wonder about it, especially at these exams. I wonder who's really on display and who's doing the strolling. It's like they're facing off across a length of glass, or maybe even staring in a mirror.

I think it's strange that, as well as being examined on diagnoses and medical management, all that stuff, they're tested on communication skills. That's what they call it. How to speak and listen to people. The history-taking. You hear them go on about it on ward rounds. *What's the story? Did you take a good history?* Like it's something you can take. Passing them sometimes, I catch the things they say to patients and I'm amazed they get any history at all. Asking what they ask in that way they do. Difficult things, huge things, all the time looking people straight in the eyes.

Like the poor waif of a bloke I brought in to see Chester in the week. He looked shocking and terrified. I didn't think he was well enough to be down there but it's never my shout. I wheeled him in and the nurse immediately turned his chair so he was right in Chester's face. Now OK, Chester's Chester and I don't want to any say anything bad about him, not after what happened that night. He's been around a while, and in his own way he does care. So how come he doesn't he get it? They all do it, talk to patients in that way and expect a history.

I collect them around here, histories, hundreds of them. Moving people around corridors, talking cheek to cheek or with my head above them. No eye contact, just our voices mingling in the air. That way, you stumble on the story rather than taking it, like happening on it by accident, caught as it honestly is.

It's how Lucy and I have our best chats, in the window

seats down at the cake shop, not staring at each other but facing out, looking at sky and trees. It's where I told her what she means to me and she properly caught it.

There was this great old girl earlier. I picked her up in a chair for X-ray. She looked familiar and she recognised me too. Turns out she and her bloke own that farm down the road, the one I run past sometimes. She asked if I'd mind taking her for a spin round the hospital before her scan. Pretend you're picking me up at my front door, she says, nice young man like you. Offers me a fag. Says she's going home today, whatever the doctors decide.

No one's asked me that before and for a second I'm not so sure. But we're early and she looks OK, so I think, why not? I give her the scenic tour and we get chatting. She says she sees me out running and asks if that was me, the other night, under the full moon. I say it was, that I'm amazed she remembers.

She says they lost a calf, that they could hear it lowing in the next field. Searched and searched, she says. So in the end, she and her Arthur and some of the neighbours – this is only a few days before she comes into hospital, mind – they move the whole herd, near enough midnight, to the field where the calf is.

I ask her why they'd do that and she tells me it's so the mum and calf can find each other. You move the whole herd, I say, move them across the fields, so you can find the lost one?

Yes, she says.

I can't stop thinking about it, even now.

Sebastian Bowen, junior doctor

Tuesday, 25 October

ARE YOU OK TO sit up now, Mr Kachnic? Seb says. I need to listen to your chest. The man nods and struggles up the bed then stops again, wheezing. His oxygen mask pulls to one side, its tubing too short, the elastic pressing into his skin.

Seb looks to the door. He could ask for some help. But the nurses hadn't come with him in the first place, had they? Even though he came to look as soon as they were worried about K. That had been the advice all along, hadn't it? Listen to the nurses, keep them on side and you won't go far wrong? But they hadn't offered to help, not as they might have done for Ben or for one of the consultants.

Ben just said, No, I'm too busy, I'll get to it when I can. He'd used that word: *it*. Not him, not Kachnic, not even K. He'd glanced up from his paperwork and smiled crisply at the nurse in the way Seb sees consultants smile when they've had enough of a patient. Seb feels his mouth repeating that smile now, practising its shape in the dimly lit side room.

He won't ask for help. He can't. What would he say? That he can't manage? How pathetic, how weak. But true, maybe? He lifts a knee to the mattress like he's seen the others do, hooks an arm under Kachnic's axilla and asks the man to push down with his heels. *One and two and* . . . he heaves him successfully up the bed.

Moments like this – cannulating a patient, say, without dripping blood on the sheets, or having someone readily agree with his decision; small, pedestrian wins – they make him feel OK again, a real doctor, like he's properly arrived. He stands by the bed and fiddles with the oxygen dial, conscious there's no real need but still pursing his lips seriously like the anaesthetists do, looking completely in control.

At the cardiac arrest last week, that anaesthetist, Dr Graham, had shouted at them from the head of this same bed, telling them off for their chaos. No frantic running, she had boomed. A tall Scottish woman with waves of hair loosening from its clips and a kind but weathered face that looked over them, like she'd seen it all before and so many times. Frantic running makes me nervous, she shouted, the patient lying beneath her, dead and waiting again for the possibility of life.

Seb's memory of it, the maelstrom of activity, comes to rest on the student, standing by and looking intently from anaesthetist to patient. Dr Graham, on positioning the laryngoscope and advancing the endotracheal tube, had turned to her and said, Hypokalaemia makes your myocardium frisky, not so good. Cool as that. Seb pocketed the phrase and repeated it that night in his mirror, summoning the student's wide eyes, the brown shine of her skin against the scrubs.

He leans over Kachnic to listen to his back, lowering the stethoscope like a probe into dark water. The posture's awkward, and his body remembers the contortion from another patient, another body in that first set of nights. They seem so distant already, but in reality were only a couple of months ago. His first few weeks as a doctor and those odd, hallucinatory nights.

During one shift, his registrar was caught up in Emergency for hours, leaving him to struggle on his own with an elderly lady's blood pressure. On returning, the registrar had snapped at him for having not called her or intensive care sooner. You can turn these people around, she said. You are here to keep them alive, you know.

After the morning handover, the daylight and warmth rising around him, he returned to his room and stayed up for hours, revising the management of sepsis. But the books didn't tell him what remained unfathomable: would they honestly have taken her to ITU? Should they have? She was so frail, so fragile, almost bird-like, weightless and blowing away. But maybe he was being too soft? Or was it too nihilistic? The idea of intensive care hadn't even occurred to him as possible, let alone as sensible. Maybe the seeming folly of it had made it inaccessible to him. Or maybe he was just being a bad doctor.

He hardly slept during the too-bright days of that August week. Some of the others would gather first thing after a night shift to drink shots and trade stories of their heroics and horrors. But he lay awake in his room, or if sleep came at all he dreamt fitfully and woke in a panic of remembering: a missed X-ray or blood test; someone's pain too quickly dismissed; a pedal pulse he was sure he'd felt but which, on reflection, might just as easily have been his own circulation echoing back from a patient's oedematous skin.

One dream repeated: that he was inserting a chest drain, but instead of pleural fluid or air, arterial blood pumped from his incision. He worked frantically to collect it into a wobbling frame of glass tubes, something he had to keep building to collect and reinfuse the lost blood back into his patient. A crowd gathered, tutting at the harm he'd done, the mess he'd made, the growing mess of blood and waste.

Leaning over the septic lady that night, as he's leaning over K now, he had rested his head on her shoulder and fallen instantly, blissfully, so briefly asleep. It was that same night that he saw the student for the first time, moving around and between patients, like a bee, flower to flower, in the faint light and hum of the ward.

There, he can hear it now, at K's right base: new bronchial breathing, its familiar sandpaper rasp. Another chest infection, the third on this admission. He steps away and looks at the man from the end of the bed: tachypnoeic, probably starting to decompensate. Should he think about calling intensive care?

The cardiac arrest had been in this very room, in K's bed and, who knows, perhaps even in these sheets, now washed and recycled. This thought, not for the first time, leaves him disorientated. Like the hospital's caught in some other sense of time. Like those quickened films where the sun and moon tear across the sky, clouds dispersing and forming, each point of traffic becoming a continuous map of neon lines. Everything hurried, so individual moments and lives are indistinguishable, lost, transparencies laid over each other so you can look through the lot of them and see nothing.

Each one held briefly to the light and then dropped, only to be replaced immediately. Is that it? Is that how things are? Important, like they feel? Or trivial, as they appear to be?

He leaves the bedside and opens the side-room door. Like breaking the seal on a glass jar – the puck of released air, the ward flooding in. For a moment he stays still, holds the door ajar and thinks how best to step out, what to say and do. He takes it all in – the ward stretching away, the day, all that might happen in it, all he might do or fail to do. The sound and the bright, hurting light.

Years of hoping for medicine, all the conversations with his family, the anticipated grandness of it all – about him, about what he'd achieve. And here he is, ill-prepared and faltering, looking onto a ward and a world like he remembers looking onto school playgrounds, like he still does these days on arriving at mess parties.

He pulls the silver pen from his pocket, places it firmly between his lips, pushes the door wide open and strides out.

Ben sits in the office, facing a computer screen, his feet thrown up on the desk and his back to the door. Seb takes in his easy posture, the pink shirt, the stubble. He's always worn white shirts himself, even as a student, always nurturing this image of a doctor: talking seriously with colleagues or called suddenly to a patient, sunshine falling on the clean cloth.

He met Ben at the new doctors' party, the night before they both started. It was apparent they'd be on the same ward and, after a few beers, Seb had reached for this man as one might for a lifebuoy, gripping firmly. He showed Ben his silver pen, the gift from his parents, engraved with the Hippocrates: *Primum non nocere*. First do no harm, Seb grinned.

I know, Ben said, how sweet. Careful you don't lose it down some giant cleavage, I've seen whole stethoscopes disappear down there, whole fucking men.

Seb laughed, raucous, grateful.

Ben quickly became the voice on the ward, the junior everyone looked to, nurses always asking where they might find him. He was certain, easily decisive and authoritative, speaking only when necessary and never asking for help or advice.

He invited Ben back for dinner one night in the first week of the job. We can have a few drinks, he said, catch up. He offered this casually but spent hours on the meal, then dishevelled his room just enough from its usual pristine state, hiding his collection of textbooks and the cards from his parents. But Ben didn't come.

Later, lying in bed, Seb heard his voice outside, the distinctive laugh. He stood and peered through the curtains. And there he was in the lane, kissing one of the nurses, hands under her blouse, her belly exposed. He watched until they went inside, then returned to his bed, carrying the scene with him, merging it with his own pictures of the student undressing in a side room, K's side room, of her looking at him and waiting.

First thing this morning, he failed again to catheterise a patient. The man in four with a brain tumour, who he remembers from previous admissions. A young man who's deteriorated so quickly and dramatically. His partner waited outside, tearful and beautiful. And Seb felt it briefly, the awfulness. How, until recently, they'd been casually living in the way we all casually breathe air. Was it this recognition that left him struggling with the catheter, the man's penis left messy and red in his hands, sodden with gel?

The nurse called Ben in to help. He arrived, ignored Seb and spoke loudly, directly to the patient. Right then, boss, he said, we're going to pop this in now. He passed the catheter firmly and easily, smiling at Seb on his way out, that same smile. Come on now, Sebastian, he said, time to man up, you might have to find a clitoris one of these days.

Seb steps into the room, clearing his throat quietly to

let Ben know he's there. K's bad again, he says. Then, after a pause, hearing and hating the doubt in his voice, Pneumonia, I think. I'll get a portable X-ray. He phones down to radiology, asks for a mobile film. No, he says to them, no, it can't wait and he's not well enough to come down, that's why I'm calling you. He puts the receiver down and mutters, Lazy idiots. Aware that he's saying this as an offering to Ben and instantly regretting it, wanting to call them back to apologise for his tone.

Losing your cool again, Ben says, hooked now and turning to face him. That's not good. What's up with you this time?

Nothing, no, I'm just—

What?

K's gone off. They asked us, didn't they, to look at him?

Yeah, and you jumped to it like a good boy. He's stuffed, Sebastian. It's pointless. Been stuffed for weeks. I'm not running around just because no one can diagnose stuffed-fucking-itis. Ben laughs. You need to stop before breaking a sweat for these girls. Forty-odd years of this, like a fucking marriage.

But he's sick. You can turn people around. Seb stumbles on the phrase, unsure he believes it. You can't just—

Can't just what?

You can't just . . . You're not always right, Ben. He hears himself pleading. Look, ethically, you—

Turn them around? That's your ethics?

Not at all. I think. We have to decide, though. Talk to him and decide. Otherwise get him comfortable, surely? I don't know what the right thing—

You never know, do you? That's the problem. Whose patient is he?

Bhatia's, I think. Seb's voice shakes. He wants to leave, to run from Ben, from K, the hospital. It was all perfect snow before he started, the idea of him, of medicine. Maybe even as recently as this morning, or before he came into the office a minute ago. The idea of him as a doctor. Now there are footprints all over it, mud and slush thrown up. He doesn't know who to be, how to be. He wants to hit Ben, to be held by him.

You've got blood on your shirt, Ben says. Clean up.

Seb looks down and sees the blood, the fine spray of it, likely K's or some other patient's from this morning. Staining the white. The white that seems suddenly so ridiculous. He looks at Ben, this faraway man, somehow untouched, untouchable. He'll see him, remember this moment, over and over, a week from now, years. How he looks at Ben, puts his pen down, leaves it on the desk and walks away back to Kachnic in his room. How he moves the man's bed closer to the oxygen supply so the tubing and elastic slacken. Sits and talks with him. Says, We need to have a talk about things, Mr Kachnic. His words sure and clear, audible now over the sound of the bleeps and the din of the ward.

Beth Harding, hospital domestic

Sunday, 30 October

H E LOOKED SICKER WHEN I last saw him by the hospital entrance, on the crossing. All those solid bodies surging around and under him, the school kids laughing, the doctors striding in. They kept their distance from him, from this dark mass of a man, but he was still thrown about in it, like he was in a current. The distance of others can do that.

When I started here, I wasn't much older than some of those kids. Back then, we were allowed to wear our work overalls out in public, and one morning, at the same crossing, some lad shouts, Nice tits, love. Cackling with his mates. Big hair, big blazer, more girl than I was. I nearly decked him right there, felt my fist ache with the thought. I imagined the blood, imagined Tony's face and wanted so much to hit it.

I was angry then, but I feel different now, after my time here and the things I've seen.

My first day, in Emergency, I heard them calling out to her. Jessica, they said, Jess, can you hear us? You're in hospital now. I looked in but it wasn't her, of course it wasn't, not my Jess. It was an old woman on a trolley, all of them moving round her in that way they do, like they're praying or calling out spirits. Stroke, someone said, she's been on her bedroom floor for days. They settled her and took her to the ward, asking me to clean up. Her skin had ulcers from the pressure of lying on it, and already, so quickly, there were larvae hatching. A nurse retched and had to stand in the corner while I mopped up the blood and the maggots.

A place of brokenness, this hospital, that's what it meant to me, right from the start. Somewhere I could hide, in the way a big city with all its lives and troubles makes you feel smaller and makes you feel OK. Jess'd say that sometimes when we were out, tanked up and screaming with laughter, the heat of her arm around my waist: Look at it, Beth, a million fucking troubles out there, we're not on our own are we?

We'd walk through the crowd like we owned it, stopping

to drink or smoke wherever we bloody liked. I'd bask in her. The pier lights waving in and out of the dark, and out there, the sea beating, big and sky black. Her arm on me.

Some bloke or other would always stop to look at her and she'd stare right back, livid, stunning. Sometimes, staggering back into my place, Tony'd be up, waiting, knowing where I'd been and who with. I'd try Jess's stare on him, but he'd just slap it back at me, then fuck me so he could feel like a man.

Lucky you, Nancy had said. Growing up on the coast.

Nancy's is the only place I still clean. I used to do extra work for the doctors, for the cash, but I stopped. I couldn't put up with all their staring, the sad old men. I still do hers, though – until lately anyway, when things have been hard for her.

Just spruce the place up, she'd say, No big deal, take any books you like, I don't get the time to read them.

I saw her on the ward recently. She always stops to talk, asks if I'm still reading and stuff. Thank you, she'd always say, and she meant it. You don't hear it much.

That morning at the crossing, he just stopped. Stood still, right there in the road. The crowd thinned away, only a few of them hanging around at the kerb to stare at him. Then the lights changed and someone shouted at him to move. The cars revved but he kept still, his face down, dreadlocks like willow branches around him. When I walked over to him it was like I'd stepped off somewhere high into thin air, like jumping off the pier when we were kids. I felt it in my chest, the flutter. Drivers were beeping now. One of them drove slowly by him, like he was a huge tree or a rock in the road, tried to edge around him. No, not him – *us*. Around us. He smelt like an open wound, like some wards do. Old fruit or maybe flowers wilting, sweetness and decay. Come on, I said. And he came with me, back to the pavement, to the world. He didn't speak but I could hear his breath, the wet in it.

On Sunday mornings, I do the doctors' mess. I come in early so it's quiet, like now. They have takeout on Saturday nights for the on-call, so it's filthy Sundays. Smeared plates everywhere, half-empty bowls tipped up and left out, clothes and stethoscopes. I was disgusted when I first saw it. It felt deliberate, like they'd made a choice of how to be, like they were practising contempt. They scribble messages on the board: *More coffee . . . Thursday night payday party . . . Someone fucking clean up*. Bread and milk's delivered for them and left outside with the newspapers but they don't bring it in. They say they're too busy or it's not their job. I've heard them, how they talk. Sometimes it's all left out for days.

Look and you can see him now from the mess window, over the road. His silhouette against the school fence and first light, leaves falling around him. The playing fields stretch out behind him, and further out, faint in the watery light, the hills rise up. Like big waves out at sea, like the ocean stopped mid swell, just before it comes crashing down.

After a while, I told Nancy all about the coast. I told her about my Tony, how I was scared to stay or leave, how one day I just walked out, then ran, got on a train and came here. I showed her the scars he gave me. I said about Jess, the pain of missing her, how she was the only other person to see these scars, to really see me.

I said the right time to visit a town like mine is in the winter. How the arcades become hollow places that flicker and echo like found caves, newspapers blowing in and out of them. How, empty of tourists and cash, the place is like a beach at low tide, left bits of life scuttling around, human beings that survive outside the brightness of things.

I told her how I like to walk the path between the rail track and rocks, trains whizzing past and the sea rising and falling like the world's breath. I said of course it'll come over us, the sea, one of these days, wash clean over us all. Why wouldn't it? And that doesn't feel so bad to me, I said, it feels OK.

It was a Sunday morning like this but in the spring, with that doctor. I'd seen her around with her mates, always in her too-tight dresses, wide-eyed, mascara just like Jess'd wear it. I knew she'd seen me too, the way she looked. It was early that morning, still night really, the birds just starting up. She'd been on call and was in the nights room just off from the mess when I came in. I knew she was watching so I moved about purposefully, keeping my back to her, my hair pinned up. I picked up her thin cardigan from the floor and held it to the light, making a big show of it, then brought it to my face and breathed in deep, smelling her perfume and sweat. So when she came in and pulled me to her from behind, I let her. Let her hands move over me, clumsy and expectant. We went to her room, and I can still see her face now, how she looked at me as I undressed her, how she saw what I saw, in her, in all of them. That I wasn't the one who was afraid.

The bread and milk they leave out, I've started giving it to him. He walked past once while I was cleaning and I ran straight out, not stopping to think. I just took what was there at the door and pressed it into his hands. So he waits every Sunday now at the same time, slowly becoming visible against the low sky. No one sees us.

The school kids go in and out of their building over the road. Mad, that it's so close to our hospital; the harm it does, showing its privilege within spitting distance of all this. Like a factory spewing out smoke and polluting the air. But none of it's privilege, really, is it? Not in the hospital or outside. It's all luck. Everything's an accident, everything's chance. So either nothing matters at all, I reckon, not a fucking thing, or else it's all enormous, every bit, like we're responsible for everything at every single second.

He was sitting outside the station the day I arrived, asking for change, one eye bruised, his lip split. I remember the pink blossom against the sky, the black of his skin under it. I said to him, OK? He laughed, threw his head right back and shouted the laughter. He wouldn't stop, so I moved away. I walked off and found myself here. Hadn't planned to, but I wonder now if it wasn't the sight of him that did it, brought me to the hospital.

I go out to him now but I'm empty-handed and he looks worried. I explain then I take his hand, like before at the crossing. I bring him across the road again but this time to our side, to the hospital. My hands are shaking as I pull open the heavy side door so he helps me. We come into the mess together and I lock the door after us. I've tidied the place up, wiped the board clean and laid the bread out on the table with butter and jam, a pot of hot tea. The radio's on in the corner and I've set it to play something gentle. The heating's on. We sit and eat, mainly in silence, though he laughs now and again. Someone taps on the door's glass then tries the handle. Soon other faces arrive, staring in and looking angry. They rattle the door and go round to try the window. I know others are on their way but no one can get in now.

She'd sat next door first, hoping to read through the notes and print off a path report. But the printer had crashed again, its red light blinking after brief, hopeful whirrs. She called IT and someone young, some terribly young and relaxed-sounding girl, said it was too late in the day, that they couldn't possibly fix it now, surely there must be another printer? Then Nancy had arrived, telling her that Freda, their woman on the ward, was set to leave, she wouldn't stay in for tomorrow's MRI, that her daughter and husband were with her and they were packing up. This news, this and the sound of the clicking printer, pushed Emily from her chair and propelled her into the consultation, unprepared and flustered.

Sorry to keep you waiting, she said, looking up at the clock and dropping into her chair, the notes flopping open on her lap. Her apology, to be honest, was in the hope of something, some acknowledgment at least. But the couple only looked at her, the man uncrossing his legs, readying his notepad and pen. She held his gaze a moment, a moment too long perhaps, then looked back down at the notes. Leafing through them, she remembered them now, of course; Mr and Mrs Chamberlain and their several, recent appointments.

She's struck, and not for the first time, by how quickly consultations are shaped. In seconds really, set in motion like clockwork or else broken and thrown off course. The wrong word or inflection, even the wrong posture would do it. Like the notional butterfly at sea, its tiny wingbeats troubling the air, which is magnified then into storms at the coast. As a registrar, she'd seen such storms descend unannounced mid clinic or even, sometimes, terribly at the bedside.

And now, two years a consultant, she feels no better at it at all. If anything she's less steady, more easily knocked about. It's as though all her other patients, all their shouldered but invisible histories, weigh upon and unbalance her, toppling successive encounters so that the day unravels sometimes like a trail of falling dominoes.

Look, Mr Chamberlain's saying, we're no wiser here, your recommendations and so on. He taps his pencil at the pad, ticks off points as they come up. He's a big man, his knees and legs pushed firmly out into the room. His wife, Emily's patient, just sits and stares, all the while sipping her tea, the clink of cup and saucer loud in this tiny space.

When had patients started bringing in tea? She remembers as a student how consultants would be brought coffee and biscuits, sometimes even in the middle of a consultation. No one, least of all the patients, would blink an eye back then. Unthinkable now, of course. But instead here are the Chamberlains, wielding their cups and pencils and angry eyes. I don't think, Mr Chamberlain continues, that it matters one jot to you what happens to my wife, then here you are running bloody late and chaotic.

The only apology Emily really owes is surely to Nancy. Lovely Nancy who cares so fully and so well. Charging out like that and leaving her next door. Awful. When would she learn to wait, just to pause and collect herself first? But the late clinic, the printer, the ward patient – it's hard sometimes to think clearly, to be the calm and authoritative doctor.

Only this morning, brushing her teeth, she'd listened to a young woman on the radio announcing that her father was being denied treatment, then an interview with a minister about rationing and resources and so on. As though every drug, every penny, has to be made available for every treatment. All the while printers breaking, then nurses, then doctors.

It had felt thrilling though, hadn't it, once? The whole adventure of medicine, despite the challenges and the fatigues? The heroism of it. *All for the greater good.* She remembers actually saying these words as a student on her elective. A beach, a cocky American surgeon, a sunshine memory, her shrugging then kissing him anyway, everything still possible.

Maybe this is how doctors and nurses finally burn out. Past their failures, their hours, all their inhaled sadnesses.

Perhaps finally it really is broken printers and the like, the accrued weight of so many tiny things.

Mrs Chamberlain first arrived with her husband a couple of months ago and has attended another three appointments since, calling and demanding Emily's secretary fit them in when really there's no space. Both in their late seventies, dressed impeccably, she with a beauty still around her mouth and cheeks, eyes that shine like dark water returning only a remnant of light. She'd had a small breast cancer removed.

It carries such low risk, Emily had said to them, I wouldn't encourage any further treatment. Because I'm old? Mrs Chamberlain said. No, well, partly, Emily said. They're toxic treatments, and the benefits are marginal, really tiny. And of course, Mr Chamberlain interrupted, there's the cost. That's not the reason, Emily said, feeling her face redden. The same feeling she has when colleagues ask how she's settling in. Like they can see straight into her, like she's not at all convincing.

As Mrs Chamberlain lifts her cup again, she imagines the warm taste of red wine in her mouth, the feel of a glass on her lips, the immediate relief. She felt this on a ward round recently and it surprised her. Of course she'd never do it, never drink alcohol at work. Would she?

A drink in the evenings is routine now, almost necessary:

the gentle attenuation of it, a feeling not unlike being under-water at the pool, the working day dissolving into echoes and faint shapes, sufficiently distant to be rendered harmless. She can't sleep without it carrying her to bed and she longs for the gently effaced evenings: lamplight fluorescing on her dulled gaze, blissfully rid of thought. She's honest with herself about it, not proud but also not guilty, seeing it as an inevitable and legitimate response, a sort of surrender as means of survival.

She watches the other consultants functioning at work or at their occasional social gatherings and tries to fathom how they survive – flourish, even – in this charged world they share. She pictures them arriving home, the front door closing, shoes and socks coming off, the vulnerability of their bare feet, how they hold whoever it is they hold.

She wondered this about Chester last week on their shared train journey to London for the breast cancer con-ference. He'd fallen asleep across the table from her, head lolling and eyes twitching with whatever it was that haunted him. No secret he likes a drink. She'd had to politely, firmly, refuse his offer of a champagne breakfast and first-class train fare.

It was the early train, light only just permitting fields and hills into the day, cattle emerging like standing stones. A young woman sat across the aisle from them, someone

Emily recognised as a student in her group, one who was missing her lectures, someone she really needed to talk to. She herself had always been such a diligent student, as an undergraduate but also right through her years of further exams.

But what does she remember of any of it? All those hundreds of facts? And what relevance do any of them really hold now, struggling as she is just to be a reasonable clinician let alone a knowledgeable one? She wasn't sure she'd sound at all convincing if she spoke to the student.

But it hadn't been the right time to talk to her anyway, not on the train, even if Jim had given her half a chance. How he'd gone on. His looming retirement, his career, his achievements, gifts he received from patients, recent opera tickets, even. Patients want to give us things, he said. They're not bribes or even thanks, more like little religious offerings, like they're securing us.

She knows he likes her, possibly even desires her a little. Was that a flirtation, that morning on the train? Was he expecting some small offering in return for his secured attentions? She'd winked at him and smiled, hoping he'd shut up. Weak men like him, everywhere in medicine, men in positions of power, fragile men desperate for something, something owed. But what? Adoration? Love, even? Sitting here with the Chamberlains, though, she wonders if, after all, she's any different.

She receives so few gifts from her patients and feels such disappointment at this. Sure, she gets the odd thank you card, but not nearly as many as her colleagues do, long rows of them exhibited on desks next to family photographs, like trophies on a mantelpiece. She sees some consultants leave their clinics over the Christmas period like they've been out shopping, all boxes and clinking bags. Last year, she actually found herself slowing down at the end of consultations, pausing expectantly before patients stood to leave. Happy Christmas. Yes, Happy Christmas.

She made the mistake of mentioning this last night on the phone to her sister. They'd been talking about Christmas and making plans to meet up over the break. Emily said something sarcastic about the whole 'gift trade' in hospitals, and her sister asked why gratitude was such a big issue for her. Smarting, Emily ended the conversation quickly. Not gratitude, it isn't gratitude. Just something – what? Some acknowledgment of contact, of connection, some affirm- ation. Or is it actually the same, after all, as the Chamberlains? Her very own sense of entitlement.

Meaningful contact is so elusive, even here in a hospital. Like speech or music carefully tuned to on some old wire- less, only to be lost to white noise again by a clumsy turn of the fingers. She's not sure she wants it anyway, not the performed contact of gifts.

She's failed entirely to make any connection with Freda Jennings, her lady leaving the ward this very minute while the Chamberlains keep her hostage in here. She's failed even to establish a diagnosis for Freda, something solid to account for her new and increasingly debilitating neurology. She feels guilty about this and is conscious of arriving now at consultations a little on the back foot, worried Freda's abruptness is actually an expression of distrust.

But she's been like it from the start, hasn't she? Cool, unwilling to engage, leaving Emily fumbling and tongue-tied, feeling inadequate and then oddly upset. Freda's never rude, never angry, not like the Chamberlains. She's more withdrawn, disinterested even, like she isn't going to be bothered with Emily or any of these tests and treatments. She's declined all offers of treatment for some time now but it's not a lack of compliance that upsets Emily. It's more that this seems part of a wider dismissal, something that leaves Emily feeling irrelevant, like a shunned lover.

Freda's husband and daughter appear regularly at her bed during visiting hours, Mr Jennings bringing Freda a couple of beers and the little girl awarding her mother with large chocolate bars. She's beautiful, the daughter, raw, clutching her doll and sporting fairy wings that twinkle on her back.

Despite Emily's efforts, she too is hard to reach, always looking away, just like Freda.

My wife's led a good and healthy life, Mr Chamberlain's saying. Do you know how much money she's raised for cancer research? Emily looks at his wife's body, thinking how it's had the smallest in-situ cancer pipped from it, something she'd certainly have otherwise carried to her grave as keepsake from an untroubled life. God alone knows what other glitches and fluctuations her flesh silently harbours. The couple are angry it's happened at all, as if someone must surely be to blame for the sheer affront of it. And well, if she hadn't demanded the mammogram, Mr Chamberlain continues, well, it's bloody ageism, it's a scandal.

Emily has always been aware of a particular feeling when seeing very sick patients, people she might known for a while who are likely entering the last few weeks or months of their lives. Like a valve closing off, separating her from their pain. She'll still work hard for them, manage them properly, but they became distant logic problems, as if in a textbook: questions of what drug to use, what support to get in, how to deliver news, the mapping of prognoses and discharge planning. It's a subtle thing, and maybe all of medicine is only ever this set of practicalities, but she knows and can feel the difference, feel the closing off, and she's wonders increasingly if it isn't such a bad thing.

But more recently the valve appears to close sooner, sometimes even on first meeting a patient. Hadn't she felt it even as she met the Chamberlains, months ago? And is this it now, her closing away from them? And why? Because she wants them gone? How difficult already, so soon in her career and after all her training, difficult just to be kind. To the Chamberlains, to Nancy, to Freda and her daughter on the ward. Simply kind, without such tiring regard for herself.

We'd like another opinion, Mr Chamberlain says. Our GP, who's actually an old chum of mine, suggested James Chester, said he was very experienced, older. We'd like you to refer us on, and we'd like to see him privately, please. We're happy to pay. Hearing this, Mrs Chamberlain puts down her cup and saucer.

Emily doesn't like them, these people, what they mean for medicine. She wants them gone, wants to say, Yes, I'll refer you on, now please take your cups and saucers and faces as you leave.

That morning on the train, the dozing Dr Chester had changed shape right in front of her eyes. From god-like consultant into an old man. She'd pictured him asleep in his own bed, curled up against whatever it was he might struggle with, a man like that. Seeing him, she'd wondered too what would become of her as the years rolled on and she aged into some version of him.

The train had curved from brilliant sunshine into low cloud, a single cut of rainbow suspended over it. She'd watched as the student looked out, face pressed to the glass, to a world that still held the surprise of beauty for her, eyes reflecting back in and staring clearly at Emily.

The Chamberlains push open the door to leave. Past them, over by the reception desk, Freda's little girl stands with her father by the vending machine, skipping impatiently, lit wings fluttering up and down, holding her doll and a bar of chocolate. Seeing Emily, she grins and throws a big wave. Emily waves back.

But, leaving the consultation and turning to look, all Mrs Chamberlain sees, walking away now with her husband, is this doctor, this young woman, smiling, waving and looking, yes, thankful.

James Chester, consultant oncologist

Wednesday, 26 October

J AMES CHESTER. TUESDAY CLINIC. Final patient: Dan
Gillespie. Mr – sorry – Daniel S. Gillespie. Twenty-
eight, five, fifty-four. Letter to GP Jack Marshall, Smith
Street. Copy in palliative care. Draft, please, and email me
to check. Thanks.

Dear Jack, thanks for referring this sixty-one-year-old
man with probable advanced lung cancer. Given his comorbid-
ities and functional status he's not had a respiratory work-up
or biopsy. He's smoked forty a day for most of his life, and
has a significant history of alcohol intake. His past history
includes alcoholic hepatitis, chronic renal impairment and
ischaemic heart disease with three previous MIs. He presents

now with four months of increasing anorexia, weight loss and breathlessness as well as new symptoms and early signs of SVCO. I note the chest X-ray and CT findings. His current medications are as listed, with no known drug allergies. I agree with your reservations around him being fit enough for any kind of systemic therapy. Our goals are manifestly palliative and his prognosis is almost certainly poor. He lives alone in sheltered accommodation where he has some friends and they, his friends—

Jack, I know him.

Why did you send him to me?

How could he come from you?

I didn't clock his name in the letter. I didn't even register it when they brought him through for the consultation. But then, honestly, I rarely do. Surely that's not just me? Even sometimes mid consultation, the notes will be next door and I'll realise I've no idea who I'm talking to. And it's not just patients, before you start having a go. You ask Maria, she'll tell you.

She still asks after you, Jack. We drifted apart, I tell her. People do. I don't hear from him these days.

I should say, He despises me, Maria, and you know why don't you, love? Anna, I'd finally say to her. Come on now, I'd say, we all know, we just never say. All the things we don't actually say to each other but secretly always know.

How we wear our secrets, openly and silently, like diseases.

And then after all this time, Jack, you send me Dan.

Anyway, you ask her, Jack. Ask Maria. She'll tell you about me and names. Say there's someone heading straight for us on a Saturday morning, our hands full of shopping or whatever, I'll recognise the face but I won't know who they are and definitely won't know their name. I'll say something like, So how're things? In the hope of a clue. Are they a patient? Or a relative? Has someone died? Are they complaining about me? Maybe they're a colleague. It's probably someone who doesn't like me very much and I should watch out. There are too many names and faces out there and we're expected to hold them all in our heads, aren't we?

But then, of course, you probably manage it, Jack, don't you? Out in GP land where you all care so bloody much.

Remember that time I teased you about it, in front of Anna? That first time I met her? You'd not been together long. Where was it? I can see still us all – the sunshine, trees, dappled light. We went rowing after. Regent's Park, was it? I remember the Post Office Tower, so it must've been when we were still at UCH.

She looked . . . I don't know. What can I say now?

You, anyway, went on as ever, maybe even more than

usual, to impress her. The GP, the patient, all that stuff; how you were the last proper doctors, the only ones who really cared. I said I didn't ever remember my patients' names, not one, but they were all doing well, thanks very much, Dr Marshall.

I can see her now, London's spring light, the freckles on her shoulders. Which would you rather, I said to her, a name or some honest attention? A rose, Anna, I said, by any other name, any bloody name at all, dear, dear, Anna.

It was then, Jack. Soon after that first meeting. And yes, I'm sorry.

Anyway, these people arrive at us on the street, humiliated that I've forgotten them. And their faces, that smile, you know, we see it all the time don't we, in clinics and wherever: the slightest separation from tears. Maria steps in, of course, always has, intercepts them, cushions us all. She has small talk on speed dial. That's our deal. All couples have one, don't you think?

This patient said to me, just the other day, that she feels most connected with her husband, most close to him – listen to this – when they make the bed together. Not when they're having sex in it. Just when they make it. Just the fact of their acquired choreography over the years. I looked at her, that she'd described this thing. Love, I suppose.

And you, today, out of nowhere, through your thick

silence from the other side of some hills, you send me the letter-bomb of Dan Gillespie.

Of course, listen, I won't post you this. I'm just talking to you because you sent him. I'm just talking to you like this, into this machine, like we do, late in the evenings in an empty office.

Like confessing, isn't it?

An NHS confession though, let's be honest. This blasted machine keeps stopping and starting. There's a whooshing sound when I play it back. Listen, here: see? Like the wind. Or waves. Like I'm shouting from the sea.

Anna did that. She called me from the coast. She didn't say much, just cried. And the sound of the sea, like a storm, like it was a Mayday. Like those accidental answer-phone messages people leave you, phones turned on in their pockets. Accidental, secret Maydays.

Like this, like now.

Mayday, Jack, Mayday, do you receive?

So when I get your letter, when I get it, your letter, I do what I always do. I pull him up on the screen in front of me. Pull up his scans. And there he is. All of Dan Gillespie on my screen. Except I don't know it's Dan yet. And at the same time it's more Dan than anyone's ever seen. Even me, with his fifteen year-old face right up against mine and his hand crushing my balls as he screams in my face.

Now I think of it, it's extraordinary how I can just pull him up this way.

How about that, then? There must be a market out there. Pick your school bully and flick through them in any plane: sagittally, axially, any way you like. Here, look, I'll show you, wait. I'll summon him up now. Let's have the whole experience. Me looking at Dan and talking to you. The whole shebang.

Funny thing is, I remember patients' pictures, if not their names. I remember the scans. They keep, like bright sunshine when you've shut your eyes. Like holding Anna that last morning, the window open, the world red and warm against my closed eyelids.

His scan was bloody awful. A huge tumour, most of the right upper lobe, nodes, clear SVCO and liver mets. A frail man with advanced cancer. Not a hard decision. Bread and butter, in fact. I'd be done in ten minutes if I was quick about it, maybe even time for some lunch for a change, if Nathan hadn't already eaten every edible thing in the canteen.

Sister came in and told me the patient was acting a little agitated and frightened outside. Could we bring him in next, she said. They all look at me wearily when they say these things, knowing I'll snap, probably worrying a little for my health lately.

You might have heard, I don't know, have you? About my scare? I love that word: *scare*. Maria's word, not mine. Be careful, love, she says. Remember your scare. Like it's someone jumping out at me from behind a door. Or a shout to stop my hiccups.

Scared, old bean, scared exactly of what? What's there left to be scared of?

Failure, maybe. That after all we amount to so little. That we squander our moments, almost inevitably.

But not, surely, of death.

I loved Maria, didn't I? I still do. I don't know. The truth feels slippery.

But you, Jack, what about you! What happened to you? Are you OK?

You were important.

I thought of you that day, the day of the scare.

I tell you, the pain was actually, after all, not how we describe it. Not the textbook weight of a textbook on the chest, down the arm, up the jaw. What kind of a pain is it, sir? Sharp? Dull? Shooting, cramping, aching? On a scale of one to ten, how bad would you say it is? Hopeless questions, I now know.

Those patients, I love those patients, the ones that settle down to our hurried history-taking, sit back, stick two fingers up to the clinic's ticking clock, sit right bloody back, cross their legs, sigh – slowly, even the bloody sigh is bloody slow – and say, Well, doctor, I wouldn't exactly call it a pain.

Well, I tell you what, mate, as it goes, they're right. It isn't a bloody pain.

Just, something, I don't know, tectonic.

I only noticed it when it stopped, like you notice when the nebuliser's turned off at the bedside; that relief of silence, how the quiet can seem suddenly loud. A couple of days later, still with the odd twinge, I thought I should get it checked out. So I head down to radiology, ask some favours and get a CT-angio sorted.

I looked at the pictures with Peter Nicholls. Smug little toad, isn't he? It's like entering a damp cave, seeing him. Radiologists really do live in the dark. They're the angels of death, not us oncologists. Dev Bhatia asked me once if I found it hard, knowing patients' futures. But actually it's them, it's the radiologists, peering blindly into us, like seers.

So he pulls up my scans and asks me to sit down. What is he? Twelve? And asking me to take a seat? Little Lord bloody Fauntleroy. He shows me the images and it's like he's winded me. There it is, atheroma in the left anterior descending. It's not especially narrowed, Jim, he says, I'd be surprised if there's any flow effect. He says I need to see a cardiologist, get a proper opinion and some more tests.

But by now I'm not listening to him prattle on. I'm staring at the bright line of coronary artery, like it's an aerial shot of a river, pinched thin by its shores, the sort of place you'd stop to skim stones.

Then again, looking at it now – I've pulled it up on my screen right now – with my head tipped to one side and filled as it is with a large whisky, that artery's close enough to vertical, narrowed like an hourglass, a whole life dripping through it.

When Dan does come in, when the porter wheels him in – I can see this now, but it's too late because it's gone with every other bit of the past – just for a moment I choose not to look up from the notes I'm reading. Quite purposefully. I've always done this, to seem busy, to seem caught up in something else, something bigger. And then, slowly, acting it out for him, acting it for everyone, Jack, I say his name and lift up my head. Just so everyone's clear that I'm important. That's what I've always done.

He's sitting in a wheelchair with Sister next to him and suddenly I'm seething – at your letter that's staring up at me from the desk, at what happened to us, at him not being well enough to even have his nails clipped and at the sad waste of all our time, Jack.

I come closer, take his hand. I can see he's lost weight, the duffel coat almost hung on his scaffold of a body, legs lost in the loose cloth of his jeans.

And she's quite right: he is frightened. Funny how bad we doctors are at seeing that. You hear us talking into it, regardless. Like we're shouting into a gale when it's obvious that all our words are being lost. I wonder sometimes if we've not felt it enough, if perhaps we should be made to feel it, so we know how to look for it and how to meet it in others.

You said in your letter he was confused, but when I speak to him he takes it all in. I tell him we might have to admit him to get him sorted out, to irradiate the tumour pressing on his blood vessel. He hears that he's sick, that we can't cure it.

All right now, Mr Gillespie, I say, I'm just going to have a proper look at you.

His shirt's open at the neck and I can see the run of collaterals, like cracks opening on his skin. Skin that's pale, almost translucent, with a sheen to it. Have you thought to check his haemoglobin, I wonder, Dr Marshall? Skin that's almost cadaverous, already seeping life. Fingernails nicotine-stained and perfectly clubbed from the malignancy. I make a mental note to emphasise that in my letter to you, to say how all of this adds up to a bronchial carcinoma, that of course you'll have noticed the obvious finger clubbing, Dr Marshall, you stupid angry fucking lost GP, you were my best friend and I loved you and I'm sorry, thank you for referring this terribly unfortunate—

Then I see the trace of tattoos across his knuckles.

My initials in olive green on his tracing-paper skin.

I stop and look up, my hand still holding his, holding it tight, and I look at his eyes.

I see him staring at me, shouting before he hits me: This fist is all yours, Chester, it has your name all over it, mate.

I lift his hand into the light from the window, hold it up like one of those old X-rays. Remember those, Jack? Back in the day. You and I competing to pluck them out of the envelope and spin them the right way up onto the light box. We were only allowed a single spin. Who was that guy, the dishy guy who did it so flashily, that guy we'd laugh at, the one the girls adored?

I must have sat like that for seconds, staring at him and his hand. He let me do it in that way patients do, like they forget to breathe out again unless you say they can. Sister was obviously troubled at my long silence, at what I was doing, and asked if she should call the ward now.

I took the call next door and told them we were admitting him. They asked why and I shouted down the phone, and,

Jack, I was almost sobbing now. To look after him, he's coming in so we can bloody well look after him.

I'm going now. I'm going to see him then I'm going to find Maria.

It hurts, Jack, here.

Sara Nicholls, artist

Friday, 28 October

IT STOPS RAINING AGAIN, quite suddenly, so I leave the X-ray building. The light appears new, like it's been washed clean in the wet air. It blinds from puddles and the slate of roofs, from the chrome points of cars and buildings. Do you remember that watercolour we bought in Venice? How the artist had left the whole of the canal paper-white? The fierce white of light on water, the ache of it on the eyes, all of it rendered as a pure absence.

I returned here that evening, after the consultation, to find Dev. Am I allowed to call it that, really, my encounter with him? A consultation? I was startled by a fox, right here. It dropped from the shadows and flew out across the dusk like a firework, like a sudden ghost. The hospital must fill with these ghosts, surely? Spilling out here and there as foxes. If I stop a while, might I see it again now? Maybe it was the fox in the end that did it, like some omen, because I didn't go to look for him after all. I thought of you and of Jon, and I came home.

Jon's already excited about firework night. He's keeps talking about it. Remember last year when he asked you about rockets, why the bang comes after the flash? You were home late and irritable so I answered, summoning what I understood from all our chats, from your physics-laden head. I said that sound as well as light must move through space, arriving at our eyes and ears in their own time, first one then the other. Even sunshine takes whole minutes to reach us, Jon, I said. So we're always seeing our closest star as it once was. Later that night, tucking him in – I don't know if I ever told you this – he asked me if that meant that all the stars that we see glittering, especially ones that might be long dead, are really ghosts?

Not just stars, I might have said. But us too, love. Bits of light reflected and arriving at someone's eyes whilst we, somehow or the other, have moved on. Like we're inevitably ghosts to one other. All our moments, shed light as much as shed skin. I sat on his bed this morning as he dressed for school and I wanted to hold us there, to seal us together in the brief present.

When you told me that first time you loved me, I didn't believe you. I was visiting you at work, making an entrance for the others to envy, to impress them for you. You said it to me in the dark of your office, kissing my neck, someone's bones flickering on a screen behind us.

I dropped you off in this car park once, the light breaking into diamonds on your shirt. You were waiting for Nathan, who'd just stepped out of his four-by-four and was walking towards you. You shrank a little, looked down at your shoes then squinted up again, squaring your shoulders. That look on your face as you stared back at our car – or was it, Pete, at me?

Yesterday, you and Jon waited for me on the downs. I spotted you first, standing under a tree, Jon's hand drifting worriedly up to yours as a dog strayed too close. Light moved in the trees, seemed to actually move them, like they were anemones in water. Branches swayed over you, like days and nights hurrying by. I watched a while as you appeared and disappeared in the shadow, like I was practising loss.

*

You were so thrilled by it all at the start: your private work, the respect of your colleagues, our new friends, your research, the parties. I remember sitting in your study once as you prepared slides for a lecture. You showed me a 4D scan of someone's chest, their lungs and their breath caught and repeating on a computer. We were talking about where to live, about schools for Jon. You scrolled the mouse absent-mindedly so we zoomed in and out of the body on the screen, like it was a window, like the pixels were stars.

Dev tried to hide it but I saw his face change when he felt my belly. When I sat up, his hands on my back, the shock of his kiss, I thought of our eclipse. We'd rummaged around that day to find my old chest X-ray. It's the perfect filter, you said. We were in the garden of our old flat – this was years before Jon. We held up the film to look through: a thorax, and past it some buildings, then the sky. Your hand in the same place as Dev's kiss, here by my ear. The half-light was strange and beautiful, as if that was all the light the world really needed, enough light to see things by and to marvel at them. And the eclipse, a pure bracket of light, pressing itself to the dark film of the X-ray. Like hope insisting. Look, you said, right in the ribs, stuck in your heart, like a bit of shrapnel.

Tom Patrick, hospital chaplain and
Nathan Munro, consultant oncologist

Thursday, 27 October

G REAT, THANKS, NATHAN. NO milk, thank you.
Some cake? Go on.

Fine, really, but thanks.

Should we grab a table then?

How about over by the window? Some light.

Good to see you, it's been a while.

Yes, and you. How's business?

Business is – well, you know. Busy.

I can imagine.

Everyone's sicker. Or more demanding.

Is that so?

We're all victims, aren't we, of medicine's success. Even the clergy.

I think you might be right there.

Everything's stretched. I know you hear it all the time, Tom, but really, it is.

Very hard for you I imagine. For all of you.

We plod on.

Lunch must be a rare treat?

Well, I make a point of stopping. A proper break.

Do you?

It should be in our contract, I say. Or in the oath. *You will look after yourself.*

Yes, somehow.

We should try and catch up more.

Yes.

There's that Italian place, the one by the school?

You'd have the time?

I mainly come here. But I'd make the time.

For escape?

Yes, quite. Trickier for you though.

This? The white collar? It glows in the dark, I'm told.

Occupational hazard?

Yep, spot on. Great phrase that. Anyway, thanks for calling about Jim.

No problem. Awful. And so close to his retirement. Makes you think.

Does it?

What it's all about, I mean.

You asked if I was praying for him.

Yes.

You pray?

Sorry?

Do you pray?

I'm not a religious sort, Tom.

Funny to hear it said out loud, that's all: pray.

In the modern world?

In this one.

I'll be sure to whisper it next time.

Yes, would you?

So how are you doing these days? Ever want to lose that collar for a bit?

How strange, why?

Come down in disguise? See reality on the ground.

On the ground!

You're too visible! I bet you never stop.

Well, look, it comes off easily enough.

I didn't mean to—

No, really, it's fine. Makes no odds. I can still feel it. Anyway, time to practise without.

How so?

My own retirement's looming now.

Of course. That must be odd. Is it soon?

A few more weeks.

Not long at all, then.

Still time. Did you know Jim and I started here together?

I didn't. So how's he getting on?

OK, I think, but I don't have a feel for it. You neither, I guess?

No, no idea. Too specialised, us doctors, blinkered by our own expertise.

Actually, isn't it your clinic now? I don't want to hold you up.

You're not.

Just I heard you were taking on some of Jim's work too, so you must be even busier.

Lunchtime. Like I said: Look. After. Self.

You're finished early, though?

I left it with the juniors.

I see.

It's the only way. They learn. The 'business' survives. I survive.

Through absence?

Only like surgical trainees 'closing' after an operation.

Closing! Like we're all wide open.

I'm impressed you know my clinic times.

Because of your young woman with breast cancer. She's in, isn't she?

My patient?

Susie Francis, yes. I meet her regularly at your clinic. While she waits for you.

I see.

You can't place her.

No, but, well, there's hundreds.

She's a regular on Sundays, has been for years. Before she fell ill.

Right.

Had the rash for months but kept it hidden.

Oh dear.

Always has a Bible at the ready.

Oh yes! I know the one.

I didn't catch her last week, I was away.

On holiday?

Just walking. Up in the Lakes.

With family?

No, alone.

You don't get lonely?

No.

I hear it's lovely.

It is. But the heights frighten me.

Really?

Always have. Proper phobia. Sweating palms, shaking legs, the whole thing.

Fear of falling?

An appropriate fear, surely?

Not at all. Come out to the chalet with us. My shout. Some quality skiing will fix you.

No, thanks. Narrow paths, big drops. Not for me, Nathan.

All heaven's angels would surely catch you, Tom.

Right.

Sorry. Naughty.

No, let's do it, let's give the faith a hard time.

Really?

I've been thinking about it, about all of us.

Sounds ominous.

Your lot, mine, what we believe, what we promise.

Our lot?

There's always more life on offer, isn't there? Then finally there's eternal life.

Now you've lost me.

That's your deal, isn't it? And mine. Prolong life.

Well, not quite.

Like we're winning at some game.

What an odd way of thinking about it. We treat diseases, and sure, we prolong life.

And you think it's important.

You don't?

It feels trivial.

What?

Like it's not enough.

Saving lives isn't enough?

It's so easy. It asks nothing of you.

Tom, I—

Look. I get that you're clever. Busy, capable. All that.

And so?

I know you can do it all, Nathan. But you give nothing.

What do you want me to give?

It's just a set of tasks for you, isn't it? Medicine. While you stay intact.

You want us – what? You want us to break?

Maybe. A little.

Come on, Tom.

Or it won't happen.

What?

Care.

Smiles? Hand-holding? All that stuff?

I'm irritating you.

Well, honestly. You're being naive.

Am I?

You want us to go through some motions? Some elabor-
ate dance?

I told you to care.

Meaning?

People, Nathan. I want you to hold people.

Right, well—

Hold them or we fail.

Tom, I'm a bloody good doctor. It's busy and it's
demanding. No one's failing.

In your version.

My version?

Not just you. We're the same.

You? The Church?

The Church, all of us really. Impressed by bright displays,
a few shiny miracles.

That's a fine way to talk about your faith.

You don't have to worry about me, Nathan.

Well, I might say the same.

Take the resurrection.

You know what, Tom? I should probably go.

We're all so thrilled by it. Someone beating death. Like
that means God.

But not for you.

Who knows? Who cares? The death's the miracle, surely?

If you say so.

The sacrifice, the love.

Ah, love. OK.

Yes.

Look, I have to go. Nice to catch you. It's been odd.

A man comes to work, delivers the minimum conception of his job and expects, what, benediction.

Me?

Oh, and lunch. *Is* it you?

What is this?

Susie.

What?

The woman on the ward.

My patient?

Yes.

What about her?

How is she?

She's in hospital. You said.

I asked you how she is.

I don't like your tone.

Have you seen her?

Not yet.

Will you?

Not now.

Are you capable of seeing another person, Nathan? Actually seeing them.

Tom, I'm asking you one last time. What is this?

You tell me.

You're way out of line. I'm done with this. Leave the medicine to me.

I do.

Good.

Her first appointment – two months waiting to see you.

Is that what this is all about?

She was frightened, Nathan. Sick.

I'm busy. I can do what I can do.

They said you'd see her the next day if she went privately.

And? And? That is a service, you know.

A service?

Private medicine, yes. A real thing, Tom, in the real bloody world where you don't live.

You had the time for it.

It's different. She was praying for—

Praying?

Paying. I've no time for—

For lunch at an Italian restaurant?

Fuck! Tom.

Why are you even a doctor?

You've no idea. About any of it. I've done nothing unethical. Or even unchristian, for that matter.

No.

You're completely out of order.

It frightens me. That you're possible. People like you. Here.

People like me? How dare you.

Just like this, Nathan.

Because you're a better man?

No, I'm a coward.

And I'm your retirement party, am I?

Will you pray for her, Nathan?

You're mad. You haven't heard the end of this.

You know that she is?

What? Come on. She's what?

Praying for you, Nathan. Praying you'll be a fucking doctor and look after her.

Radha Sethi, medical student

Wednesday, 26 October

THE STUDENT WATCHES THEM as an anthropologist might. She'll stand sometimes at the hospital gates, pretending to wait for friends, watching the staff arrive. She looks for patterns in how they transition from the world to the hospital, noting shifts in gait or changes in expression, the occasional unguarded response when they encounter patients. Sometimes she waits in the clinic reception to watch the day's activities unfurl, like a market being set up, or a fair. She watched Dr Bhatia come in this morning, how he and the nurses moved towards and away from one another, like charged particles, the combined force of their stories pulling and pushing them into a dance.

There are only a few months now until finals. And though she attaches herself with ferocity to ward rounds, clinics and the like, she misses all her lectures. She knows her way precisely around the patients, but much less so the facts. She finds the facts tedious. She thinks of Dada and his jazz. Medicine feels like this. Like she can improvise the notes but doesn't care at all for the sheet music. Surely she'll be found out? Surely she will fail.

Her insistent, quiet presence makes her as familiar as she is invisible. So she moves freely around the place, unchallenged. She surrounds herself with bodies and persons, inhales them, not only the patients but also these faltering and broken nurses and doctors, the porters, even the chaplain. They give her something.

In her wanderings she learns the building's landscape, like learning anatomy and its subtle variations. She sees its repetition across other hospitals, like the one in London where Dada is. Patients and relatives flounder in this space. It's opaque to them, and chaotic, their illness projected onto every corridor and confusing sign.

Nurses and doctors walk easily around it, with intuition and an odd grace. She thinks if they were dropped into any hospital, anywhere in the country, perhaps anywhere in the world, they'd orientate and move with certainty and freedom, marching brazenly into wards and departments,

owning the geography. What is this ownership? A land-
lord's right to the space? The privilege of knowledge, like
a cartographer? Or is their sure-footedness somehow a
statement of mastery over sickness and death, like they
police the borders?

There are two new doctors on her ward. It's clear they're
both terrified. Ben – the cockier, the prettier – is flippant but
flails around fearfully. She's drawn to him like she might be
to an animal injured at the roadside.

He spoke to them all a few weeks ago after the ward
round about breaking bad news. She hates the phrase, pictures it as a scrolling TV newsflash. *Breaking: bad news.*
Maybe one day technology will alert us in this way to
everything that breaks in and around us, to the loosening
of glaciers and cells.

Ben said to them, with all his three weeks of clinical
experience, that they should crouch down to the patient's
bed to deliver the news. He smiled like a TV medic, fixing
them with the gaze of this hard-won insight. She caught his
eyes on her body. Not everyone wants that, she said, it's
belittling. Why not just speak to them like they're people?
A nurse called him away but she lingered as the other students walked off.

*

She gets the early train to visit Dada in London. She goes alone, lying to her mother and brother that her studies make it impossible to coordinate with them. She closes herself off from their cinematic grief. She can picture her mother returning to friends' afterwards, shaking her head in hurt affront rather than actual sadness, her eyes pained for the camera. *Hey Ram, Hey Ram.* Her brother standing by; his doctorly stature. Is this what Raj is really like as a GP?

She hears Dada's voice echoing to her from years ago: the things he'd say, the poetry he'd recite when she came home from school in tears, uncertain. *We had the experience but missed the meaning!* He held her, laughing loudly, as he shouted, Elioootttt! A long, drawn-out cheer, as if the dead poet had just scored a goal.

He's less well now, though the nurses say he still has good days. Ate some breakfast yesterday, didn't you, Raj? Their voices change key when they speak to him, lengthening to a sing-song, as if his dying might be rendered in nursery rhymes. She watches their mouths move, their heads tilting to one side or the other, like automatons with the key turned, or children playing. Their *ahhs* and their *oohs*.

She reads to him before leaving. *All the darkness of night exists in the depth of daylight.* He would read her this Tagore once, opening her curtains to let in the night as she sat combing her hair. He pronounced it *poym*, not *po-em*, his

Hindi accent thickening the word with something the English never could. Longing, music, the simple heat of bodies.

She pronounced it like this once at school. *The poym I will read.* The class shrieked with laughter, even her teacher. She never told Dada but was livid. The arrogance of it, as if there was a single and approved way of translating the world, a cold and dead way. She thinks the same is true of medicine, of training as a doctor, and she runs from it.

We had the experience but missed the meaning. It's only now in her twenties, visiting her dying father, that she understands he is real. She recognises that for all their years together, all her love, he's only ever amounted to a notion, an insubstantial cloud or figment of hope. But now, suddenly, in the centre of his illness, he's revealed as discrete and as solid, quite remote from her. As she sits by his bed, the idea is overwhelming, this truth of his separateness. Resting a hand on his, she calls to him over and over. Dada, Dada.

One morning, earlier in the summer, she was calling to him in this way from across the house. He took up the chant and repeated the syllables, telling her again the story of Shiva's drum. Fire in one hand, Behti, drum in the other, destruction and creation, together, no? A drum beat to end and to begin things, but the same dance. Da Da. Hum Hum.

Om Om. He massaged her head, percussed it like a tabla, beating his truths into her.

Visit by visit, he transforms in front of her, the life cooling around and inside him, like a planet forming. He solidifies from idea into person and now, increasingly, into flesh. Two weeks ago she sat staring at him uninterrupted, the curtains drawn around his bed, as if he was under a lens: the papery creases at the corners of his eyes, the hair in his nostrils, the silver curve of his nail beds. Where his pyjamas fell open, the staccato lift of his belly, thin-skinned and tense. His breathing more laboured and erratic, the concertina of his ribs darkening with each inspiration.

Watched so closely, he appeared vividly and obviously an animal, a limp creature found in the woods, all hair and fragile breath. She looked around at other patients. Lying in beds, sitting on chairs, walking with frames and stopping at toilet entrances, drip stands or catheter bags in their hands. The texture of their skin folded like hide across their faces; the pure physical substance of their bodies. The same for the nurses at the desk. She tracked one of their varicose veins with X-ray clarity, through the blue uniform and pink flesh, all the way back to her pulsing, waiting heart.

These people, these bodies, their erosions. She just wants to be among them, learning them with her hands. Asked on ward rounds to examine a patient, she's fluent and easily identifies the signs. Dr Bhatia demonstrates findings and pathologies to her. He shows her how to percuss for the dullness of an effusion. Lift your hand, he says, like a pianist, then drop it. You'll feel the note before you understand it, see?

She's skilled at procedures, thrilled at the contact they afford, particularly cannulation, even the most difficult veins that have thinned to the width of cord. She enjoys the press of a needle tip through a vein's wall and its movement through the pinned vessel, the dark flash of blood. She's astonished by the simple fact of blood. Before labelling the bottles she holds them up, light from the windows filtering through them over beds.

Dust gathers in this light, in a mezzanine over the ward's hum, the shed skin of doctors, nurses, patients and students suspended and mixed over them all.

The other students grow close, drinking together, falling into cliques and brief intimacies, a huddle against this world they've encountered. She goes back with Ben one night to his room. What does he want? He's incapable, she thinks, of love. He kisses her and she allows it, fascinated by his longing. Pushes him against the wall, holds him until he is hard and makes him come, watching his eyes as they close. Open them, she demands of him, open your fucking eyes.

They all meet outside their digs on payday nights and tonight she decides to join them. At the pub she listens to them talking about their days on the wards, events and patients traded like commodities. *Done four of those . . . the pancreas . . . cannulated three . . . a diastolic murmur . . . so this overdose comes in yeah?* The giddiness of words. Shrieks of laughter. How close this hysteria is to fear. It makes the same sound.

She leaves again, almost immediately, walking through the rising carnival of the pub, blinking at faces that are hardening through laughter and drink into grotesque masks.

The night is sudden, star-sprayed, too wide to care. Walking back to her room, she crosses the hospital's car park, the building lit up like a ship pitching in the dark, all the windows bright. She cuts through Emergency, the sounds of bleeps and yells, drunken cries and shouts for drugs or obs. Two nurses are frowning by a computer. A young doctor reties her hair in a bun, pen in mouth, eyes darting. Trolleys fill with a mess of bloodied greens. And porters' radios echo messages as if from across the world.

The arrest bleep sounds. People turn and move, gather pace. The call is out to the car park and someone swears at this odd summons. She runs with them out into the corridor.

The anaesthetist spots her, red bag over her shoulder, grins at her. You again! Come on then! They burst into the night, running, cold air slapping their cheeks. This way, they shout, come on, over here, in the corner. Their footsteps drum loudly. *Da dum, da dum.*

She sees the body and shouts, Dada! But her voice is barely heard, taken by the cold and the pounding feet, the drums, such drums, all around her now. It isn't him, of course not, she knows that, but she recognises the man. The others do, too. Bloody hell, it's Chester, someone shouts. They pull open his shirt. A doctor starts pressing at him, like he's pushing him into the earth. She sees Seb, the other doctor from the ward. Looks at his face. He asks her to cannulate and she does this easily. The drums deafen her now, silencing the rest of the world. *Da dum, da da dum.* Why can nobody hear?

Hannah Burton, medical secretary

Friday, 28 October

I ACTUALLY WENT OUT WITH a Seb once. Back in the day. Pompous arse, he was, not like this doc. Funny though, how names come back to haunt you. I grew up here so I know a lot of the local ones.

When I was younger, if I gave the doctor some notes or letters to sign, I'd say if I recognised the name, if there was some particular story, an affair or whatever. I was showing off then, trying to impress. It'd feel like a betrayal now, giving away stories like that – histories, as they call them – just for a pat on the back. Other people's stories are precious and not mine to give.

But the thing is, this lot love a gossip. Though they'd

never admit it. Ha, can you imagine? *So why do you want to be a doctor? Well, mainly I love all the gossip.* And it's not just the stuff about one another, it's about the patients. All that jostling, I hear them, the 'long chats'. I've had a long chat, they'll say, with the wife, they've not been getting on for years now. That sort of thing. Sometimes I think there's a smugness to it. Like they feel better about their own lives hearing the mess of others'. Maybe that's the whole attraction of helping people, I don't know.

I wonder what they'd make of my story if I turned up sick tomorrow? What they're making of Jim's now? I'm not having a go, definitely not at young Seb. Like I said, I can't thank him enough for bringing me the tape. And then for coming back to check on me today. But I'm OK now.

I am embarrassed, though, by being such a show-off back then. Even though the doctors were actually unsettled when I told them those things about patients. Funny. It's like they felt less important all of a sudden. You can still hear it in their voices sometimes, the waver in them. Like they're reminded there's a world out there that the rest of us live in, us and their patients. Like they're just visitors. I know they like feeling important, but actually most people just want to belong.

I worked on switchboard once, my first job here. You got to know people well then, better than today. Every August the new juniors would arrive. From miles away back then. Proper, actual visitors. There was this Scottish doc. I liked him a lot. Drove all the way down from Inverness and right on to his night shift. They wouldn't cope with that now, would they, not this generation. I hear them in Jim's office complaining about missing their breaks. Jim's never been like that, all the years I've worked for him. They could learn a thing or two. It's always been about the patients, even though he joked and ranted about it. Sorry, *jokes*, I should say. *Jokes and rants.*

It was great on switch. We could be young and silly and OK about it. I flirted a lot, everyone did. Harmless enough on the phone, I'd say, just voices, just words. That Scottish one and I ended up talking loads, right from his first night. I never met him though. Funny to think of that now, the odd intimacy of it. A good solution, I reckon, for struggling love. Sit yourself in a dark room and just talk. No touching. He told me about his long drive down and how all the juniors, all over the country, moved from hospital to hospital on exactly the same night. Like a trick, he said, like pulling away the tablecloth or spinning the plates.

I worked nights then, the money was better, me and this girl Lisa. She was trouble. Leading them on with her breathing and whispering. It was terrible but really funny to listen to, her grinning at me and winking all the while. This was long before we were ever recorded – you wouldn't get away with it now. She said she was doing the place a favour, bringing in a bit of love. But if you listened to the doctors, they were lost, far away. And she didn't give a monkey's about it, you could hear that.

That's the thing about voices. I've listened to so many, all the tapes and phone calls over the years. You get good at reading them. I think our voices hold their own alphabet, like a code. Patterns that hold the real meaning of the words and sentences, of the mouths that speak them. If you just read a sentence or watch a face speak, then you carry away a version of the thing, their spin or your take. But close your eyes and listen. Then you hear the pure fact of it. Voices don't lie. They can't.

Take Munro in our office yesterday, telling us all about Jim. I've some bad news everyone, he says. And even then his voice stays hollow. How must that be for a patient? Important words offered as empty sound. I stood at the back of the room and watched him as he talked at us. That pale, tall man. Like a winter tree. As I fainted, there was this bird on his shoulder, singing loudly into his ear, telling him it was spring.

I was sick on the carpet. The girls helped me back to the office and sat with me a while. They brought me tea and tried to send me home but I said I'd be fine. We're all dispensable, Jim said to me once. The waters close behind us without leaving so much as a ripple.

I wanted to go and see him, but even the thought of it . . . Just the thought of finding him shored up on a ward. That's when Seb came, with his Dictaphone and the tape. It's JDC's, he said, from the car park. I didn't want the letters to get lost.

Funny how we abbreviate them into their initials like that, into just a few letters. Like cramming genies into jars. Same as they do to diseases. CVA, CUP, ACS, all the acronyms I type. Shrinking the thing into something more manageable, I suppose, something to hold in our hand at arm's length, something less problematic.

I've listened to that tape over and over now, his voice. I keep listening to it and retyping it. I have it here, folded up in my hand, and I can hear him in it, speaking to us, calling.

Lucy Conway, staff nurse

Wednesday, 26 October

L UCY FEELS FOR THE lump again, here over her
clavicle, just at the muscle edge. As a student nurse
on ITU, she'd watch as doctors placed tracheostomies near
this, always shocked at the proximity of a body's breath to
the outside world, the ease with which a needle took it. Or
how easily blood was drawn from here, the sudden trick of
it in a syringe, a central line's wire advanced, the cleanness
of it done well.

But ITU hadn't been for her, much like surgery. The
whole palaver of them. She was hopeless anyway at staying
sterile, always scrubbing incorrectly and even having night-
mares about it: standing in theatre and washing her hands

raw then knocking them on the tap or sink, having to start again, then again. This was her place, this job, here on the ward with actual patients.

She does miss the blood though, its open visibility in theatres, the pedestrian presence of it and the remarkable honesty of that. Funny that venous blood's always coloured navy in the books when actually it's a deep, dark red. The colour, surely, of Homer's wine-dark sea? She said this to her anaesthetist last year on their walk and the conversation faltered instantly.

They'd arrived at the top of the hill and he'd quietened. But why? Was the poetry not 'nursey' enough? Or was it just too much for him? But too much what? So often poetry sets people on edge. They say it's too sad or too soft or too emotional. More likely it's just too true. Too true anyway for a doctor. He'd advanced a kiss to fill the silence and she'd returned it, but only half-heartedly, all of London beneath them, its breath held for his grand and imminent career.

They happened on the pigeon on their way back down. Bloodied, its wing broken and pointing to the sky, so that Lucy followed the apparent gesture and found herself looking up. Her date – this being their first and, as it turned out, only date – said they should kill it. Right away, he said, given the injuries. It's not salvageable. It was the first time she'd heard the phrase, but she's noticed it a lot since. *I don't*

think you can salvage him. We could do a salvage mastectomy.
That sort of thing. A terrible word, she thinks. The wrong
word for matters of life.

But he reached down without further discussion and
gripped the bird's neck, triggering it into a violent thrashing,
almost a kind of seizure. The wound opened wide and the
sound of feathers and squealing surrounded them. Seeing
it, he staggered away. And Lucy stepped forward, lowering
her foot then all her weight onto the pigeon's head, pressing
it into blood and grass and mud. It was over quickly, the
afternoon quiet again, the sunshine on them warm.

She thought of this the other night, undressing and
pushing her work shoes, as she always does on Fridays,
deep into the back of the wardrobe, her ritual to bury the
week. Was it some smell that reminded her, some musty
remnant of London's summer on her clothes? It was then,
held in memory and crouched by the cupboard, that her
neck hurt and she found the lump.

She's not sure if it's grown a little. Has it? It's quite small
and surely completely innocuous. And she feels so well. She
can lift it, just, between her finger and thumb, like a pearl,
and roll it over the edge of bone. If someone were to pass
now, they'd see her standing at the open doors, her face to
the garden and back to the ward, hand raised to her neck
like she's surprised or enchanted by something.

Church bells snag on a breeze, then fall. A skin of broken cloud perfectly demonstrates the earth's curve. With her eyes closed, this autumn morning feels indistinguishable from spring. Two pigeons applaud the air, startling her as they clamber through it to a high branch. How improbable, the flight of pigeons. She closes the doors, turns to face the four-bedded bay, her three patients and, past them, the rest of the ward. All of it, so improbable.

The TV on the wall is muted as it plays a hospital soap, more pantomime than drama with the sound down, all the gestures heightened. A doctor and a nurse look gravely on from the bedside as a patient coughs up blood, their eyes fretful and deliberately sad.

Lucy silences the alarm on Mary's IV then turns back to the screen. That's not it, she thinks, not it at all, not that charade. Anything felt – on the rare occasions it is – is just happened upon, accidental rather than chosen. It's often the fleeting recognition of an actual person in the body of the patient she faces. The feeling passes quickly but it leaves an ache, and for a while everything that follows is filtered through it.

The TV scene changes to the patient and daughter being given bad news, the camera lingering on the woman's face, her hands fluttering at her eyes. This gesture again, she sees it all the time now. Is it really intended to dry tears? Or is it a distress signal, hoping to draw attention to them? Perhaps it's only to summon tears where in reality there are none. She saw a junior doctor do it the other morning after a night on call, sobbing at an apparent first encounter with death. Why the fat tears, Lucy wanted to ask, it isn't your loss.

This bling of tears, casually adorning the hospital. Like emojis reflecting against the painful truth of things. The hill, her anaesthetist, his face aghast and recoiling from the clean fact of a suffering bird.

There had been another time, another anaesthetist. She was still a student in Emergency when an elderly lady was brought in semi-conscious with widespread burns. It was clear she wouldn't survive, not even the night, that she'd be dead in hours. Lucy stood next to the doctor as he spoke into the woman's ear. We're going to put you to sleep now, he said, get you fixed up, you're going to be fine. The lie seemed effortless and therefore all the more shocking.

Would she be so surprised today? It had been a kind lie, but aren't they all? Here, anyway, in a hospital? Kind offerings to soften the sharp edges of life. But the lies, these days – on the wards, on the telly – seem more insidious, nuanced and harder to tell from the truth.

Mary stirs, breath whistling, from a fitful sleep. Still tachypnoeic, but her blood pressure and urine output holding up. Maybe she'll settle. Maybe, as the night doctor put it, she'll 'do'. But then what? Everyone knows she's dying, vacillating across the grey line of it, but still they won't stop all this. It's like they can't.

The doctor had chastened Lucy for giving more opiates. The same young doctor in fact – almost a little girl, Lucy thought – who'd sobbed at her paper-cut encounter with death. The accusation – handed down from her bosses and the wider profession – was clear if poorly articulated, premised on medicine's biggest lie. How its main goal is to prolong life. How not to aim for this is a sort of failure, caricatured otherwise as soft, like palliative care. If not culpable then certainly not proper, manly medicine either.

But then look, here Mary is, actually a little brighter again. Fighting? How often does she hear that? *Of course I'll fight it.* An endless battle where the stakes just aren't clear. I'd fight, Josh said to her, I'd fight for you, if you were sick. They were in London, walking by the river before a show, the light falling and the water under the bridge polished by it, the river moving towards and away from them at the same time so she felt, for a moment, giddy.

All the people, so many people, thinning in the dusk, faces bleeding into it, becoming it. They passed a couple, a man pushing a woman in a wheelchair, NG tube visible at her nose and taped to the cheek. That's when Josh said it, that he'd fight.

She wanted to tell him this weekend about the lump, about her worry, that it might of course amount to nothing at all. They were in bed on Sunday morning and she was about to when he jumped out for his run. He stood dressing in the room's sunshine, limbs moving in and out of its yellow square like he was covering himself in paint. She watched him. It was lovely, just to watch him. In their time together, he'd become lovely.

The night before, she'd lowered her body to his, her thighs splayed out and her head to his chest until her muscles ached. She'd listened to his heart, not just the sound of it but the felt tap. How is it possible, she thought, to hear this in a stethoscope or to take someone's pulse and not to feel something, some wonder, almost some fear? A heart beating this way for the whole of a life. The precariousness of it, the insistence.

In the end she didn't tell him. She was frightened, like everyone else in a hospital, the patients, the staff. Everyone she berates for being untruthful. As long as her words were unspoken, the possibilities they held remained undisturbed and locked safely away.

And then Nancy found her this morning. Lucy was helping in the men's bay, washing Richard West with another nurse. Richard, who'd been a runner once, like Josh. She washed his back and his legs, her hands moving on his body, it occurred to her, exactly as they might on Josh.

Nancy peeled open the curtains and asked her how Richard was doing. And then, staring straight at Lucy's neck, at the site of the lump, and with such kindness, she asked how Lucy was getting on. Like these were the same set of concerns. Like here, behind the curtains, were two patients. And this had suddenly seemed fine.

Nathan Munro, consultant oncologist

Friday, 28 October

THE DOORS SLIDE SHUT behind him, sealing off the hospital from this wide dusk and its odd warmth. A summer's night, almost. Like he's stepped from his shed onto the lawn or like he's on holiday somewhere, shoes off. He sees Sylvie, a hotel room, her dress falling. Pictures it standing by a window, straightening his bow tie, his face ghosting over rows of workbenches and test tubes.

He peers in. It's like an art installation, he thinks. A glass garden on display in a hospital window. Now that would be something worth having, wouldn't it, an actual one. Trees and bodies sculpted from glass and pushing up. Something that said to staff and to patients: *Life's breakable, but tended well, tended properly, it will flourish.*

The cleaner's reflection passes and wakes him, her distinct uniform and curves. He turns to call her but she's gone already into the building. He wants to know why the bins aren't being emptied lately, but decides he won't follow her in, not now. He'll only end up late for the Chamberlains otherwise. And only end up spoiling this moment, his perfect exit just now in a dinner suit to that audience of staff and patients.

But we ought to parade for them more, he thinks, especially the patients. Display some of medicine's glamour for them. An old boss of his, what was his name, used to say, Show them some leg. He was always stopping off on his way to parties or balls. Doing his Sunday rounds in full pinstripe regalia. Waistcoat, pocket watch, the lot. He used to tell patients, mid consultation, about his personal tailor, how he had him taxied him over from Oxford at huge cost.

There was something of the maître d' about him. Courteous but clipped. Perfectly groomed and perfectly withdrawn. And it was like he was handing them a CV with his stories. The résumé of a busy, wealthy, authoritative man. They loved it, the punters. Loved him. If anything, they were intent on pleasing him.

All the media noise these days about doctors' salaries

and status, it's all madness. This is exactly the version of doctor that people want and trust. It actually makes them feel better. If it was a drug it'd be clinically indicated.

Some years ago, quite by accident to start with, his own private-patient waiting list grew a little. And what was notable – and surely was no coincidence – was how on the back of this the numbers of patients asking to see him privately rose substantially.

It's no big secret. The more elusive or expensive or glamorous a medical opinion, the more hope a patient invests in it, the more trust. He's convinced of it. Desire and trust are so perfectly aligned in the practice of medicine.

But you have a swagger, Sylvie had said to him. You have this proper doctor's walk. The only sort of doctor, she said, whose hands she'd want examining her body.

It was spring, a bright afternoon flooding his office and the door closed against interruptions. She'd come with the usual data sheets, branded pens for the secretaries and some decent lunch for him. But also, this time, an invitation. They were asking him to deliver the annual lecture – tonight's lecture, in fact.

There's this dinner afterwards, she said, but we could always tear off to a bar. I'll put you up, of course, they've such fabulous rooms with these huge baths. Leaning against his door, she had one foot lifted from its high heel and resting on a painted tiptoe as she lamented the dullness of most doctors, how they lacked his panache and drive.

Her dress draped her like some stone veil on an old sculpture, there more to demonstrate than clothe her figure. And momentarily it had seemed possible, hadn't it, that she might summon him over, might lift the fabric so her bare thighs were pressed to the wood, that she might pull his hands onto her.

So he inhabits the swagger more deliberately now, why not? Striding out tonight through the car park or passing Dev in the corridor the other morning. Poor Dev Bhatia, face always creased into some sadness, some or other lingering doubt. Imagine having to encounter him in a consultation. Imagine, as a patient, having to encounter any number of these colleagues of his.

He despairs of them. Their dress, their demeanour, what it is they present to patients and to the world. Their lack of fire. No wonder medicine's going to the dogs. He pulls open the car door and, as if to assert the point, throws Edith Chamberlain's notes firmly onto the passenger seat.

Driving out, he notices Sara Nicholls in her car and wonders if she's been sitting there a while, leaning back with her coat still on, staring out, waiting perhaps to collect

Peter? Her expression, so fierce and distant, reminds him of their consultations. Examining her once in clinic, he'd commented on the excellent cosmesis of her scar, and she'd asked what a man like him could possibly know about scars, the depth of them.

He takes the longer route out along the ring road to miss the traffic around the fair. He should get a good half hour with the Chamberlains before driving to the conference. He announced it this way on the phone to them last night. I have a lecture to give, he said, but I can swing past on my way over, how would that suit you?

They were grateful and clearly impressed. That he was giving this talk to other doctors and that he'd actually make the effort to visit them at home first. They'd been so worried about the appointment, with Dr Chester being off sick, poor fellow. But how wonderful, Mr Chamberlain said, that we'll be seeing you instead, the top man.

Patients say this – their lower lip pushed out and with a deep, parliamentary nod – to assert a kind of hope. That all will now in fact be well. That the right man has their back. That he knows his stuff, no nonsense; that he can fix people, and keep them alive. And patients want life. He accepts they want quality, symptom control, all these things.

But ultimately they want to live. And why shouldn't they? Isn't that what medicine's for?

So much sentimental chit-chat these days in hospitals, missing this simple truth. Ludicrous, the time given to such banter. Conversations that drift so far from the hard algorithms of life-and-death decision making. Like Tom ranting at him yesterday over coffee, completely losing it. He feels furious about that, furious that his time's being wasted with these conversations at all.

But he's better off out of it, better off developing his own corner and his own practice. Sometimes in clinic or on ward rounds, he'll picture himself standing in the garden at home, weeding and pruning and planting tirelessly. A good gardener is meticulous and yes, frankly, at times brutal. But in this way, growth follows, and life. The measure of the good – at work and in his garden – lies in the outcome. And for that you need vision and you need guts.

He realises now that he's lost. Just thinking about Tom, about all of it, has left him distracted. He pulls over into a lay-by to get his bearings. Gets out onto the pavement to check a street sign against the map on his phone.

The air's darker, cold and grainy, the evening sedimenting onto buildings and junctions, changing the landscape. He hears someone shouting and turns to look across the road. Some men gathered smoking outside a pub. One points at him, says something to his mates. Raucous laughter rises between them. Laughter, no doubt, about his suit.

He stares at them then steps slowly, deliberately, back into the car. He turns the ignition but doesn't drive off immediately. He makes a point of waiting. He looks at them again. Sometimes he'd like to tell strangers like this who he is. Say to them, One day, that tumour you're nurturing, it'll be me medicating it, so show some bloody respect.

He turns out of the lay-by, sounding his horn loudly as he does so. One of the men lobs something at the car, some food perhaps, hitting it with a thud. He drives off, heart racing, hands shaking. He's just minutes away now. These closely packed terraces and car-lined streets will soon open into the Chamberlains' neighbourhood, its leafy avenues and gravel drives, the church on the green. He must collect himself before meeting them. He turns on the radio. Music fills the car, an aria.

There's a crowd ahead on the pavement outside a house. He slows over the speed bumps as he passes them. More people gather at an open front door, clustered in its rectangle of light. Heavy bass music reaches the car and mixes oddly with the radio's sound. They stand drinking from cans and talking animatedly. A little girl runs between them, hiding then shrieking with laughter. Fairy wings rise at her back, pulsing with light. A few of the revellers stand apart, further up the road, drinking and dancing. A woman sits in a wheelchair amongst them, smoking a cigarette. The road levels out and, as he changes gear, the girl lands excitedly at this woman's knees, and kisses her.

He watches the scene recede in his mirror, becoming pieces of light – the door, the cigarette, the wings. The evening is darker now but, above it all, bits of sky cling remarkably to daylight.

Agnes Graham, consultant anaesthetist and James Chester, consultant oncologist

Thursday, 27 October

IT'S LOVELY TO SEE you with your clothes on, Jim.
Lovely to have them on.

It's a better look on you.

I've never had a girl say that before.

It's in our contract, as you well know, to smile sweetly and lie.

Bit early for this?

A whole generation too late, pal!

Wait, hold on. I need to be sat up for you, Aggie Graham. Blimey.

And how are you feeling?

I wonder how many times I've asked someone that . . .

Stupid question, I know.

What's the point of it? It's not answerable.

What was that poem? You read it with us? *How are you? Fine, fine?*

'Dream Song'?

I have tears unshed. What is it? *There's a loop . . .*

Here near the bottom of my chest a loop of cold.

I have a gang of old sins unconfessed.

Just so.

I loved that poem, you know?

I'm impressed, old bean. How many years is it now? Ten?

Fifteen.

That was your first job, wasn't it?

You bloody know it was, James Chester, you old bastard.

It's not often a junior doctor says they're in love with me.

Not often, indeed.

OK, never. Never one as lovely.

Have you ever meant that about anyone?

Once or twice.

Anyway. Much, much water under that bridge.

You're not over me already, are you?

Get over yourself, pal!

I think I might be.

I was so green. So bloody green. About medicine, all of it. Life.

That's the problem, though, isn't it?

We ought to be prepared more.

Six years not enough?

Not as people, no! Not to get us good enough as people.

A lifetime's not enough. Look at us all.

It's not OK though, is it? Being such messes, I mean? For the patients. Don't you think?

I don't know. Depends. Maybe if we saw it more.

Do you still do it? Read poems with them?

With the juniors? Hardly, these days.

No interest?

There's rarely the opportunity. Never anyone around after five.

That's not just medicine though, is it? Did Tom tell you? About the ordinands?

He came over, but no.

Christmas falls on a Sunday this year and they don't feel they should have to work it.

Bloody Christmas.

Quite.

It's revving up in here already. Stirring everyone up.

How's that?

This guy in clinic last week, family hunched round him. Will he still be here at Christmas, doc?

That's just them hoping, though.

Oh, come on, Aggie.

What?

OK, let's have it. Let's have the anaesthetic take on hope.

I haven't got one. Just the human take.

That being? Hope for life, I guess?

Amongst other things, yeah. It's precious.

It's a finite resource. There's not enough of it to go round.

Says the man I rescued from a car park so he could even have this chat.

But if you hadn't saved me, it would have been fine.

You're an arrogant prick, Jim.

Fine, I'm an arrogant prick. But it's not an arrogant thing to say. The hope's arrogant.

Come on then, let's have the oncologist's take on that.

I'm no spokesperson for them.

Let's have yours then. Whatever you are now.

Just that we live our lives like we're bloody owed it all.

Not that we're owed it, Jim. But it is a gift. You especially should be thankful for once.

OK. Well. Thank you.

You can sod off with that tone.

No, I mean it. Come on, calm down.

Bit late for that.

I really mean it. Thank you. Thank you for saving me.

You're welcome. It was awful.

Just funny that it was you.

There was a whole bunch of us. Everyone stressed out that it was in the car park.

Sorry, I'll find a nice field next time.

Next time, indeed.

See him? Over at the nurses' station.

I recognise him.

Maria'd not long left yesterday when he came over to talk to me.

How's she?

Oddly fine. Wants me home. Says someone has to put the bins out.

The bins are your job? That's a revelation. Your man Nathan's been kicking off about his.

His bins?

No one's emptying his office bins and he wants to know why. Big emails, everyone copied in.

Pretty boy Ben Ashcroft over there reminds me of our Dr Munro.

Pretty, indeed.

He wanted to know if I'd like – how did he say it? – if I'd like to have CPR.

He said it like that?

Like it was a jar of sweets up on a shelf.

How are we still having the conversation like that?

You're the hope peddler! You know very well we are.

But that's just saying the wrong thing. That's not bloody hope.

Except you hear it all the time. We promise stuff so flippantly.

Yes, OK, I know.

You have to give them something to hope for, Dr Chester, people say to me.

But Dr Chester, he says no.

What's it got to do with medicine, I say. I can do what I can do and I can try to be kind.

Hope's not your problem?

It's not truthful. And it makes for bad medicine.

I get all this gush nowadays from the medical school. About the humanities?

I bet you do.

You used to say to us though, didn't you? How they teach us to use words?

Poems, yes.

We're missing the right language, aren't we, the right words for it all.

I'm not being ungrateful. I promise. I just don't buy that version of hope.

For anything?

I'd like to do the bins again.

Liar.

I love it. The evening, the rattle of them. You get the whole sky to yourself for a bit.

Simon says that, about our garden. Tries to get me out there.

He's a nice guy.

He is.

Good. That's good, Aggie.

It is.

Nathan's a bit of a gardener, you know?

Nathan of the bins?

Ha! Wouldn't that be something! If that was his legacy. It'd be apt.

Actually, I was going to say it's the other doctors who are struggling with it, not me.

With?

Me being sick. Much more than I am.

Yeah, but you see that all the time. Remember that obstetrician a couple of years ago?

Jones? Yes. What happened to him? It was something bizarre.

He was hanging shelves, Jim. Fell and hit his head. Huge bleed.

Awful, I remember.

He was on the unit for weeks. And some of the stuff we did to him.

That you wouldn't normally do?

Well, exactly.

No one's ever spelled it out for me though. Why we do things differently for medics.

We feel we owe them something. Owe ourselves.

Isn't it just more of the whole *why me* thing?

What, disbelief?

Yes, that it can happen even to us.

Maybe.

And that it can be so trivial. I mean, come on, Aggie, hanging shelves. Meaningless.

What, not like the long, brave fight with cancer?

Don't get me onto that.

They looked terrible, Jim, the team crouched around you the other night.

Funny to imagine it.

They're actually fond of you.

I doubt that.

You shouldn't. They found your Dictaphone, by the way. Gave it in to your secretary.

Nancy Wilson, nurse specialist

Wednesday, 26 October

I OPEN MY EYES AND stare at the window. Five a.m.,
green bedside light, a scatter of stars. I lie still then prise
myself up, damp with sweat. Harry stirs next to me. What
time is it, he says. Early, I say, Go back to sleep. I don't
touch him, just leave the room.

In the shower, the sound of rain all around me, I remember
the edge of my dream: Richard, a storm, insects on his scar.

I cycle to work through the last of the night, the moon
still bright, cut sharp with a glimpse of winter. A pigeon
snaps its wings, drops then rises in arcs over the shine of
roofs.

*

At this hour, even the hospital is still. Everything carries on behind walls and closed doors, in wards and operating theatres, but it's like the building's caught between breaths, waiting. I stop at the ward. Once, as sister here, I could tell how bad the night had been and the shape of the shift ahead just by walking in. Like knowing a pulse before touching the wrist.

The curtains are pulled around Richard. I pull one back and look in. He's been rolled on his side by two nurses and one of them is wiping his back. They're like children at the beach, searching under a rock. His skin has the texture of clay; the wet, hard sand of his buttocks, sheet creases pressing into the oedema. The nurse washing him is gentle, attentive. She looks up at me, name badge rising into view at her neck.

Won't be long, she says. Do you need to see him? She's young, pretty, a comma of brown hair dropped to her cheek. I want to reach in, tuck it away. I ask how she is. I look back to Richard. Thanks, Lucy, I say, I'll come back later.

A note on my desk announces his admission: *R. West. Admitted Tues 25/10. Diarrhoea, raised ICP.* But Martha had texted me the minute he came in. They'd laughed at this when we met, texting. How cool's that, Richard said,

No, wait, not cool, sick. The play on *sick* persisted, dropped regularly into conversation, not irritating because it was him, always making me smile.

And these two persisted, didn't they, somehow? Past all the others, all the other patients. This young couple, spotlit in the crowd, entering even my dreams.

That first day, a year back, walking in after his operation, it was like they weren't compatible with a hospital, their casual beauty at odds with it; his hair a flame, red and defiant, the clean line of his scar. A week post craniotomy and already he was out running. The race for life, he said. The actual one, you know.

We all fall for this, us nurses and doctors. We might comment, might say, I'm not sure how well he's coping really, that sort of thing. But actually we're seduced. More than that, we long for it. We're grateful for patients like him, the way they take the weight.

We sagely shake our heads at people's rages or consumer demands, the more usual manifestations of their fear. But we brighten at this one. How it throws an arm round our shoulder, walks us out of the hospital and shows us something else. Look, a fairground in the night. Richard found it effortless, and we all fell for it.

*

I was there at their first consultation with Emily Carroll. *Consultation*, now there's the wrong word for it. I don't mean Emily, especially; I mean all of us. The same old hackneyed phrases, repeated and tired from use. *Palliative . . . one or two years . . . not cure . . . treatment . . . hope . . . risk . . . uncertainty*. Like we're actors delivering a script.

Listen and you'll catch us sometimes – tired or just plain bored – confuse our lines mid chat, even switch to the wrong script. Just the other day, a doctor was taking consent for some small operation. His patient asked a really straight question about wounds or anaesthetic or something. And, quite on automatic now, the doctor goes, Yes, yes, that must be extremely hard for you, I'm sorry.

It was funny. A flawless performance: grave expression, deep nodding, the works. Just the wrong script. He bounced back well enough. Doctors do. Just watch Jim Chester and some of his recoveries mid consultation. But I don't know. What are we about? The perfect recital, or something messier and truer, improvised for this moment and this patient?

Martha sat still right through that meeting, the slightest frown punctuated by sudden, precise questions. Her long skirt folded like plumage around that slight body, a freckled arm resting on his thigh, hand half open to the air, as if in hope.

I watched them both, school teachers in their thirties; in

love, I assumed. When did they last wake to a normal day? When was the last unblemished moment of life before he described a headache to her? What would she say to him now, to this beautiful and breaking man? She indulged his humour but even as I watched she changed in front of me. Starting to grieve. Suddenly parental. And yes, visibly, already livid.

Everyone was captivated by her. Her beauty. Is she his girlfriend, they'd say. Awful, isn't it, not fair.

We're drawn to the young and the beautiful in hospitals. We flock to them. We meet them differently to the elderly, say, or the obese, the vast majority of mentally and physically fraying persons that fill these buildings. We prize our relationships and moments with them. Like they grace us with something, the blessing, almost, of being briefly important to them. I wonder if we're shocked too, actually frightened that it's possible for even the beautiful to come to such harm, so quickly and flippantly.

Maybe that's why our doctors are drawn to being glamorous. Like the registrar I saw Richard with last week. Hair up in a bun, bare legs and painted lips glowing seductively in the hospital lights, her black cocktail dress exposing steadily more of her as she leant in to examine her sick patient. As though, at some level, we really do believe that beauty renders us invulnerable to suffering.

But maybe that was the draw all along. After all, so many weeks and years pass, hundreds of patients, sometimes beautiful ones. My connection to them might be meaningful, but it's brief. Then, honestly, gone and forgotten.

Maybe the draw here was the fact of their beauty and breaking. That I could see her spinning away from the moment I met them. That this was a demonstrable truth, a commonplace and pedestrian pathology, like his temperature or the mitotic count of his tumour under a microscope.

They arrived at my door at the time of Harry's affair. He came home one evening, the late summer all around us, the radio on and me cooking and told me about her – her name, what had happened – weeping pathetically and saying it was over.

All our years of marriage and comfort, then this sudden new place, both of us passing through days and nights together like strangers, fearful of one another. That's when Richard and Martha came, as I clung to the precipice of days and work.

That night after their first consultation, our own bodies tired and wrinkled, Harry flailed over me like a grounded fish. I wanted to grab him by the shoulders, shake him and

— and I sit by his bed. He's exhausted, just from the effort of being washed. He seems comfortable though, the sheets new and folded, crisp light at the window, simple things. I touch his hand through the glove's latex. He looks at me and actually bloody winks. Clumps of red hair lift from his temple and his cheeks swell. His weak leg points away from me under the sheet, heavy and leaking fluid, his belly purple with bruises.

I noticed these on Monday when I visited them at home, bringing new equipment and a script. Richard was on the settee, dragged down into the cushions like his corner of the room held a different gravity. His shirt hung loose and there were the bruises, from his anticoagulant. He caught me looking. Inkblots, he said. Or fortune-telling tea leaves. Go on, Nancy, have a go, tell me what the future holds.

Martha called me into the kitchen, shouting down the hall to him, Just getting some help with the tea, Rich. She'd lost weight and her eyes were red. He won't listen, she said. He won't see it. She said he was tripping on the stairs some nights and she'd found him in the early hours, lying on them, retching and crying. She'd been frightened, hadn't known who to call.

Words poured from her. I reached for her arm but she stopped me. This morning, she said, in our bed, Nancy, the sheets were soiled and he had his hands out, covered in shit, calling me in, asking me to kiss him. I can't now, she said, I don't love him now, please, Nancy.

We discuss him at our multidisciplinary meeting, review his scans and management. Games of poker, these meetings. Decisions traded like bets, pomp and kudos thrown around like chips over a gambling table, endless posturing. *He's two neurons short of a synapse, that one. She's so fat you'll have to operate just to get her in the scanner.*

I'm not a child; I know the realities. But the way we speak, soft-skinned men and women dolled up for a night's partying – we're people who understand so little of real pain.

The registrar stands to answer her bleep, her thighs flashing, hips swaying slowly across the room. I've seen her on call, how she talks with the nurses and some of the families. Petulant, like a child, giggling with colleagues in the corridors about texts or nights out.

Eyes track her body to the door – the small of her back, her legs, her buttocks. Ridiculous, this lust. This desire for organs of shitting and lactating and pissing. One of the men grins, winks at his mate over the table.

I walk to him, nearly trip, my heart pounding. Slap his face. It's a fucking hospital, I say. Go out there, go look at the bodies, then come and stare at her.

People jump up. Voices rise around me. A chair tips back. Someone laughs. I hear my name spoken, turn, face them all and stride out.

The day passes in stills. I call some families, do a domiciliary visit, then leave early. Cycling home in the half-light, I pass a fairground and think of Richard.

Harry opens our door, lets me in. I press my hands to his, bring my head to his face. Listen, I say, listen now. It doesn't matter now. I hold his hand and bring us back in together.

dance, I said – the frightened one – have a cigarette, nice lad. But I have to be home now, I told those girls. Mermaids, I thought, ha! Nurses, I know, yes. I was saying about Arthur, the farm, now, doctor. He'll want me home. He's no good, not alone, that's my worry see. Do you think, I don't know, but will my breathing settle? That's the thing, even now just talking to you it's bad. But I was saying – no, not to you. A nurse, is she? Is she a nurse? Dark hair, lovely girl, dark eyes. I'd like those eyes for a day to see with, see what you all see, eh? Yesterday I said to her, at our age and all, you don't expect to still be alive, both of you, be around. I didn't expect to meet him in the first place at the dance, the girls were joking I'd be alone, not to meet – ha, don't you laugh now, doctor, don't you start. Look, you know. You do, you look like you know, just, what do we say about it, love, I suppose. They were joking, my sisters, everyone, was it them? But how? Are they here now? They're not, are they, in here, the girls? Teasing Arthur? No, but, no. But he was there and soon we just – this was only last year. No, it was longer, yes, much longer. So I'm not frightened, of what, well, nothing. What's there really to be frightened of, Da'd say. Nothing to fear, Mary, love. A strong man, too strong, not free ever from his fucking strength. Sorry, not for you to – you come up here to speak to me and I know what you mean but just get me home now. Listen, they were in here last night, those mermaids, asking about us, how we'd manage. We'll manage fine, I said. I told them, come round, we'll show you the fields from where we sit. There are deer now, you know, further out. We saw them on the road, on the roundabout, like the fields have inched out, doctor, into the town, like they're everywhere now. Don't keep me, doctor, not another day if you can. I haven't another day for you.

Jane Flowers, hairdresser

Monday, 24 October to Thursday, 27 October

HARD TO KNOW THE time of day. Waking now, what is it? A nurse walks around and there's a kerfuffle in the bay. Mary again, I bet. Sleep comes and goes. Like being in the back seat of a car, those long sunshine drives as a kid, head flopping on the stem of your neck.

Show me the moon, Mary shouts, all tangled in her nightie and tubes. Show it to me and I'll believe you then, open the blinds.

Not the moon again, Mary, the nurse says. Let's get you sorted out first, come on it's late. Same nurse as yesterday, gorgeous Lucy with the dark hair. I'd like to wash it for her, like to feel the weight of hair again in my hands.

They cast big shadows from Mary's lamp, like they're sitting round a camp fire. Lucy laughs her big, high laugh. That surprised me to start with, all the laughter in here. Some empty, some nervous, a lot of it – the loud, leaking shrieks – terrified. Fair play though. How else would you get by?

But I like the sound of it now; it reminds me of the salon and that I'll be out of here soon.

Jane. Jane.

I open my eyes and Lucy's by my bed, whispering me up. Has time passed? Is it still today? She's behind a deck. She's about to play a set just for me! How cool is that? We need a dance, Mary and me, maybe even Bible-bashing Susie. Lucy tries but no sound comes, nothing at all. Then she lifts out some tablets and hands them to me in a paper cup. Just your painkillers tonight, she says. Of course, the drug trolley.

Where's Mary? I ask. Then, louder, What day is it? She doesn't answer. Did I speak or just think it? She's the same age as me, I reckon, maybe a bit older, late twenties. We could be mates in another world. She walks away, out of our small light, back into the corridor and the ward.

*

This little sun hangs on the wall over Mary's bed, a wobbling circle of light. It's a bit freaky, like it's a spell or something. I turn to look for one over mine but a cloud passes over and Mary's vanishes.

I'm not a superstitious girl, not even religious, really, not like Susie in the next bed. But things can feel different in here, like everything's less solid than you thought it was.

My pain was really bad yesterday. Half asleep, I saw that old film clip with Moses and the sea peeling clean open. That's how the pain is, like my belly opening up, waves and waves of it.

I was little when I watched that film the first time. Cross-legged in the front room, mouth open, yellow Sunday light and Mum at the door in her red dress. The window's behind her so I have to squint up. She brings me a cheese sandwich and a glass of milk. Seeing Charlton Heston on the telly, she says, I watched this when I was a girl, Janey, it's great. She kisses my head and goes out.

Mary's at the window when I wake, a darker shade against the night, like she's a black hole, or a stencil with the stars sprayed round her. I can't tell if she's facing out to it all or looking in at me.

*

We're waiting for the ward round when it starts to rain, big drops pattering the garden wall. Any minute now it'll be more water than brick, wet redness freckled with dry pink. That's how things change, like you're spun around and can't tell which way you're facing, like there's only now.

I look at the wall and I tell Susie my Moses story. I turn to her and she's smiling like there's some big secret, like Moses is her best mate or something, but she'll let me have my moment. So I look back out of the window at bruised sky.

She prays a lot, Susie Francis, sometimes loudly, especially before meals, which is funny because they're slop. She dresses like we really are going clubbing, like if Lucy actually had dropped some tunes the other night, who knows what might have happened?

Waiting for the doctors now, she's in this low-neck tee and hot pants or whatever, all tanned legs, clutching her Bible and smiling at me. You can see where the tumour inches up, like a creeper at her collarbone, like Dad's roses against the fence at home.

She's fit and it's hard not to look at her. I see the male doctors and the physios doing it. Eyes flitting to her legs, her boobs, the cancer.

They see me first this morning, check my wound over and say, Looking good, Jane, looking good. Like they're passing my desk at school and I'm drawing a picture of a house or something. They say maybe I can go home tomorrow.

Then they pull the curtains round Susie. One day, some day in the future, we'll have sound, sight and smell-proof curtains, swishing round our beds like spaceship doors. Not these things, these nets that leak us to each other.

No one ever pulls them right anyway. The other day a nurse pulled them round bed four, but exposed Mary in the same movement. Left her on full view, naked on the bed and having a wash. She loved it though, shrieked with laughter, jumped up and waved her arms around. Susie told her to stop but she didn't care.

Her body's all wrinkles and lines like a map, white and thin, except her belly with all the fluid in it. Sea in there, she says, Can you hear it? Throws me a wink. Did I tell her? Have I told her my story?

I listen to the doctors talking to Susie, see bits of them through the curtains. The tests are fine, they say, Which is good, but we're none the wiser about your strange turns. They're OK, Susie says. I keep telling you, I'm healing. I can see her legs on the bed, her knees drawn up, the curve of her thighs. She runs her hands up and down her shins like she's polishing them.

I watch the doctors leave, see them roll their eyes when they're back out in the corridor. Really? I want to say to them. Come on. I've heard you lot: *It's hard to believe this or that*. Or, *We imagine this might help*. That sort of thing. You've got you own faith, I want to say. Same as her, same as all of us. A place of belief, this.

Sometimes, Mary looks like she's about to tell me something, but she stops short and veers off. The doctors find it too easy, talking to her. They're too relaxed.

It's hard to know who's who, what their codes mean. ST this, FY that. WTF, more like. Some really should have that on their badge. That's the look they have. Hello, I'm the WTF doctor. Not *I-don't-know-TF-answer* but *I-don't-know-how-TF-to-be*.

They say Mary like *Meh-Reee*, coming up loudly on the *Reee*. Like they're shouting to her. Like she's a little girl high up and too close to the edge. Like they're warning her, telling her to be more careful.

There's this one guy, Dr Bowen, who comes in every morning past the glass doors. Talking and nodding to himself. He stops outside and takes this yellow book out of his bag, flicks through it, all furtive and worried. It's such a little book, like a pocket dictionary. Is that really all they need to know?

Apparently it takes six years to train them. I did that flouncy one's hair and she told me. She went on a bit.

They all do; I hear them. They could do with getting over themselves and listening more. I could teach them that – a couple of days in the salon would do it.

That's all people really want, I think: to be heard. They can tell when you're not listening. I can tell with this lot, when they're bored or thinking about something else and want to move on.

But not Dr Bowen. I saw him with Mary the other morning. The garden doors were open and she was on the bench, legs crossed and gown fluttering. Smoking a fag like a movie star.

D'you want one, she says to him as he goes out to see her. She hands him a cigarette and puts that smile on, like she's just met him down the pub. Might as well, she says. Not got long, and it's lovely in the sunshine. He smiles, like he actually might, and they chat.

It's early and quiet, sky the colour of a silver coin. Or maybe it's dusk with the dark coming in. Is the day opening or closing? I nod off to the sound of a bike whirring past and a picture of my pink wall blossoming raindrops, like they're rising up from inside it, each one becoming a rosebud at Susie's neck.

*

She asks if I like cutting hair or if I find it trivial now I'm ill and all. No, I say, and I mean it. We're all dressing up, aren't we, all the time, for a big night out? Thing is – I don't tell her this and anyway she's gone back to her Bible – it's not just my hair I've lost, but the feeling in my fingers too.

I love the feel of people's hair. And they like being touched. They don't admit it but they do, especially the men who come in. You might think it's to do with sex, because we're all glammed up, but it's not. More about being touched in this world where we're all apart. We do that to people at the salon, like they do in here. But we do it when they're well, that's the difference. Anyway, I can't feel things any more.

Where I work, crossing the road outside, it's like crossing the world. One side's all trees and sunshine, then it's pound shops and litter, teenage mums. Like in here, moving through worlds in a few steps and moments. That's how it is, getting sick.

And then there's everyone in here. All of us, I mean. Both sides of my road meeting, like the hospital is that crossing, everyone coming in from both sides and jumbled together. Same beds, same toilets and dinners. And after a bit, I tell you what, we all look the bloody same.

*

A rave wakes me. I ask them to be quiet now, don't they know the time? Then I think, stuff it, I'll go down and join them, have that dance. The crowd pours in, all into Mary's place. They gather around her bed.

I sit up.

There are bleeps and shouts. I try to call to the nurse, but my mouth's so dry. Others come into the bay, right up to Mary's bed. I can see her between them all. Retching – no, heaving – for breath. The curtains come around and swell out with light, like a lantern.

—quick. Where's that ECG? Eighty of frusemide. Can I get a blood pressure? Some nitrates. Here, access on the left. What's the story? Bloods have gone. Someone get me the notes. An ABG? She's desaturating. Who knows the history? Is there a ceiling? Why's she in? Is that ascites? Wait, is this advanced disease? OK, I think we should stop. I've got the notes here. She's not making much effort. Is there family? Look, she's – OK, look at that CO_2. Stop bagging. Let's set a driver up. I think it won't be long. Let's—

I watch her through the night, the oxygen piped to her through thick white tubing, like she's underwater. What driver won't take too long? Is it code for something? Would they really do that? I didn't speak up for her.

In moments of sleep, she appears in a tank of water, hands tied by tubes and wires, turning around like an escapologist, calm but not surfacing, not yet, looking back at me through the glass.

In the morning she's sitting up, drinking tea in bed. That Indian doctor stands over her and says, We were worried about you last night, Mary. Not *Meh-Reee*. Looks like we've taken that fluid off your lungs, he says. It must have been frightening.

You frightened, doc? she says, chewing on some toast, winking at me.

Her belly's huge now and when she's slumped back in bed you can see her head over it, like Dad's picture at home of the earth rising over the grey moon.

They say I can go home for sure tomorrow. That they'll sort me some transport. When the ambulance brought me in, it had just stopped raining and the sky was all big clouds and drifting blue. They lifted me high up so they could wheel me into the back of it. I could see out over Mum and Dad's heads, right down our street.

It was the first time I saw — rolling backwards into the

ambulance – how you can look straight through some of the houses. That the windows line up so that facing the front bedroom you can see straight out the back to the sky.

It reminded me of that summer we were in Cornwall. Dad has this picture of me holding an ice cream. I'm all teeth and squishy eyes with my big camera smile on. Behind me's this house with the door wide open and through it there's no rooms or nothing, nothing solid, just the sea.

Tom Patrick, hospital chaplain

Sunday, 30 October

O NCE, WHEN THIS WAS still a ward, these windows
would open only an inch or two. They allowed just
a narrow strip of world to breathe from, like an air pocket
in a flooded cave. The dirty glass shielding against falls or
jumps. Such heights, after all.

He liked visiting this ward especially, being around the
elderly patients. What happened here felt like a barometer
for the whole of the hospital.

One Sunday – Effie still little and skipping in with him
after church – the sunshine seemed to congeal in here.
Patients dozing in it or propped up like insects in honey.
He'd wanted to force the windows open that day, break past

the latches and push the glass panes wide out. Like they are now. For sky and air to flood in through the bodies and do their work.

What had provoked that? More than just a bit of stale light, surely? Something said at church that morning, he imagines, or more likely left unsaid or not meant at all. Something, in any case, igniting him. As it had with Nathan. Pathetic, to still be so buffeted by people, to be tipped into a rage.

But then to what end the Church's genteel composure, its bloody indolence?

Beth pointed to it that morning after his sermon, pointed right into him. Like she'd plucked a stone from his belly and held it out on a palm. Here, Tom, she might have said. Look at this, sedimenting inside you.

He'd been asking after Susie and she'd told him. About her health, about the appointments with Nathan Munro. She said how – because of his terrible behaviour, his terrible indifference towards Susie – she'd stopped emptying the bins in his office. That there was only so much dirt she was prepared to hide away in a hospital. What's the point of you being there, she said, if doctors like that can carry on?

But his row with Nathan had been pointless, hadn't it? Nathan's actions – or rather, his inactions – were completely legitimate, clinically and legally. He's found that doctors can, and so often do, deliver just the bare bones of medical treatment whilst not giving a damn about their patients. That this is an accepted norm of medicine.

The plaster in here is dry now, paling incrementally over his many visits. The workmen never stop him coming in, the benign old chaplain. The electrics will be fitted soon, then some paint and office furniture. Desks replacing beds, keyboards tapping where footsteps once hurried past.

But it's apt, surely, that the managers are housed in here. It has a symmetry to it. That they sit where bodies once ebbed, their sharp suits caught in the ghosts of patients.

It deserves a prayer, a loud one every morning, like an imam's. First thing, before the computers fire up. A prayer of reverence for the place. Surely for all place. Is there a place that hasn't held, or mustn't one day hold, some or other suffering?

It'd take, what, a second to fall from this window to the ground? He remembers watching something once, a science documentary explaining how a feather and rock fall in a vacuum at the same speed. As if the differing substance of us is similar to the eyes of the world, all of us gravity held and bound.

All heaven's angels will catch you, Nathan had joked. A

breeze lifts and he grips the window frame, his sweat-filmed palms wet against the wood.

This had shocked Effie on that walk over the summer. Dad! she'd yelled over the press of the wind. Your hand's soaked! She'd taken him out on the coastal path, like she was showing off her new property for his approval, her new life.

The track had thinned as it rose from an inlet, the perspective around them widening quickly into one of exposed sea, the landscape tilting. He'd asked her to hold onto him. He'd never asked that before of his now grown daughter.

He'd almost been sick that afternoon, the vertigo worse than ever. But why? Is this all just an effect of his ageing? Like the decline of some chronic illness, say, or wrinkles deepening with time? Or might it be actually that he is just more frightened these days?

Walking home last night, things already felt unsettled around him, after that whole business with Nathan. And, on reflection, perhaps it was simply that: an upsetting encounter colouring everything that followed it. But sometimes it's like the world's thin veneer cracks a little, exposing heat and brutality. As if – an old phrase of his, and he can see Jim chuckling – as if the devils are out.

He'd passed through the park, which was alight with a fair, a dozen or so rides and some stalls. Couples, a few families, clusters of teenagers. Two girls, young women really, screaming as a ride brought them low then carried them out again. He watched, thankful for the cheer of it.

Then one of them pulled up her shirt so her breasts shone in the strobe. She called to a gang of boys at the duck shoot and they hollered back, an animal sound, the tallest one thrusting out his pelvis, teeth green in the light. Surely just schoolboys, wisps of facial hair and rugby shirts.

A family passed and he watched the silent stand-off between the father and this teenage lad. The man staring hard whilst gathering in his kids. The boy only looked back, as if the children were invisible, or worse, irrelevant, not just the fact of them but what they meant. Cocking his hand into a pistol, pointing it and pulling the invisible trigger.

What if it had been him, standing there with Effie? Years ago, her mouth sticky with candyfloss. Would he have lashed out at the boys? All hope of kindness, his or anyone's, lost in the face of fear?

He remembers being on the big wheel with Effie once, singing to her as their seat rose, silencing his fears and preventing hers. At the bottom, lifting the safety bar so she could jump off, he saw a bee drop from it. A single dark snowflake. It reached her cheek, and stung.

*

WHERE, O DEATH, IS your victory? Where is your sting? Who said this? Just the other day. Someone reading at a funeral? No, it was spoken to him, presented right to his face in a corridor somewhere. Someone grinning. He can see the man's expression, arm around his wife, both of them smiling. Expectant, victorious. Like they were presenting a proof or evidence of something. It was that elderly couple, well turned out – the Chamberlains, was it? – stopping him in Outpatients.

She'd had breast cancer, but look, she was doing so well now, they were saying. Their faith had brought them through. But nothing prepares you, does it, the man said. And why Edith, of all people?

They'd seen Dr Carroll and were waiting for a second opinion, he announced. From Jim, it turned out. Did Reverend Patrick know him, he asked, This Dr Chester?

Why do you lot insist, Padre, Jim had said to him once, that we're made of any more than just particles? You cause us all such trouble. Years ago this, at some party in the country. Leaning in, invincible and glorious in a white shirt and sunglasses, sipping his drink.

They'd not long met. He'd asked that Jim get him in to watch some undergraduate teaching. And he'd sat in as students dissected a rat's heart. Looked as they suspended it from thread and injected it with drugs, the life in it coming and going, stuttering out in rhythms which they recorded, it seemed to him, with a confused rapture.

I don't give a damn what we're made of, he said to Jim, Just what we do. And science won't help you much there, mate.

Jim sat back, that bloody smile on his face, and their friendship opened.

He emailed Jim for advice about Nathan and the appointments with Susie. Don't make a fuss, came the reply. His behaviour's completely in line with getting a bloody chair, or a knighthood, and we wouldn't want that now, would we?

So after the row, he'd gone to look for Susie on the ward. To absolve himself, he supposes now. Of pig-headedness, of stuffing it up so mightily. Like parishioners sometimes do, confessing things, an affair or whatever, then offering some charitable donation. As if there really is a cosmic balance we can square for ourselves.

People must believe it. Or otherwise, faced with their pain and loss, they wouldn't always present him with that same question, voiced or not: Why me? As if to say, I deserve this less than others. Less than the damaged, the seething poor, the insignificant and damnable many others.

Jim wondered if doctors believed it, too, or at least a

version of it. You hear them, he said, superstitiously wondering if a particular patient mightn't do too well because they're far too nice a person.

But anyhow, Susie wasn't to be found when he got there. Her bed was empty, just a Bible splayed out on her pillow and the rest of the bay quiet. Two patients asleep and the nurse, perhaps Effie's age, looking for a moment out to the garden. A newsflash played silently on the wall-mounted telly. Pictures of a dinghy at sea, refugees in the water, children crying.

He'd drown instantly at sea, for sure. In a swimming pool he's coughing in seconds, swallowing and inhaling water, static despite his best efforts. It's a long-running joke with the family, and Effie laughed at it again when they stopped for sandwiches on their walk, light scattered around her like parcels on a dappled stretch of path.

She talked about her work, about climate change and the reports of diminishing Arctic sea ice. You'll be in trouble, she said, when the waves come in.

The thought of it has always frightened him. Nancy told him once how the clergy are often the hardest patients to settle when they're dying. Terrified, she said. You ask the folks up at the hospice when you're next there.

*

Voices rise from below, someone shouting, a commotion under the trees by the door. The heads of a crowd visible from here, like they're bobbing about. He pictures it for a moment, the ocean beating at these hospital doors, people awash in it.

He closes the windows, leaves the old ward and sets off back down the stairs.

Someone will have to clean up this stairwell now, for the new arrivals, the chief executive and all the suits. Look at the state of it, cobwebs and ivy creeping in through window frames. Like he's descending into some mythic jungle, what with all that noise and shouting outside.

He stops and looks back up. It would make such a chapel. Set high like that – beds for pews and the windows wide open, there at the top of the hospital. Somewhere a congregation would have to climb or be carried up to.

The voices crescendo now, clamouring outside the stair-well door.

A large crowd clusters around the window and door of the mess, knocking at the glass and shouting in. Someone calls for security on their phone. A man arrives with tools. Is someone trapped or hurt? It's hard to see over all the heads.

Has something happened? They've bloody locked us out, a young doctor says. It's out of order.

He looks in, the room appearing then disappearing amidst the jostling bodies, through the glass. A woman's sitting at the table, laughing. Beth? A man faces her, his wide back to the window, his hair wild, brown hands holding up a piece of bread and breaking it carefully it in two.

Radha Sethi, medical student and Sebastian Bowen, junior doctor

Thursday, 27 October

IT RAINED LIKE THIS once when I was at school, he says. I looked up just as it started to fall. She turns away to the window, the watery evening, the lights mixing like paints on a wash of street. She's surely tired of him, he thinks. But even if it amounts to just this, just a few days, an hour even, sitting with her on this bus, even if that's all . . . And maybe he's being too fanciful about the rain. But he wants to tell her, to give her what he saw: a net of water shimmering for a moment between the sky and his face.

She reaches a hand over, threads the brown lines of her

fingers between his, and returns him to her. The contact sets an old thought ticking. What really is the last bit of him? The furthest out particle of him that becomes the first bit of air, or the outermost surface of whoever he touches. He wondered about it holding K's hand on Wednesday. How we're more penumbra than wall, where we end and meet.

The rain made a stream along the kerb that day, he says. Me and some of the boys raced matchsticks in it. It was summer.

He doesn't say it was the best day. The only day he felt any belonging at school. That, seeing him later, his mother just scolded him for being so careless. How, still now, in a hospital, belonging seems such an elusive trick, performed so easily and with panache by everyone else around him. Until the conversation with K and until these days with her.

Have you ever seen the monsoon, he asks.

Yes, she says. We spent every summer in India with family. It's like the sky's been tipped. People laugh and run through it. It's warm, so heavy. She remembers a dog run over in the street. Levelled steadily into the tarmac like a length of wood being planed down. Then washed away in the rain, just like his matchsticks.

She'd sit with her cousins out on their roof in the cool evenings, watch kites nod beautifully for attention over the city's teeming life and death. She'd like it, to fly a kite with him in the orange blue light.

Their bus is locked in this traffic. The driver reads a paper and the wipers beat time. Someone on their phone says there are deer on a roundabout and that the road's blocked. Voices always flying around this bus. When she sits with the others, travelling between tutorials and ward rounds, it swells with voices, patients' and doctors' words running immiscibly around each other, shrill and disconnected.

A mother's voice, over at the front, catches her ear. We'll dry you down, love, she says to her daughter. Soon as we're back home.

She turns to him and says, A man said just those words. About his wife. Wednesday on the ward, before our night. He said to me, Jean would always dry me down after my bath. I stopped scribbling his history down and looked at him. Imagined her pressing the towel to him, like blotting paper. After all their minutes and years and intimacies, still that. She might have kissed him – mightn't she? – even a proper kiss. He told me she died in the spring, all matter of fact, like he was explaining about his bowels or his appetite. Said he'd outlived so many people now – friends, even children. It was an odd thing, almost funny.

Last night, in her room, after the events in the car park, she told him about her father. Asked why we ever feel grief at all. As if it's a surprise, she said, that they die, the people we love. He wonders how Dr Chester's doing. When they took him round on a trolley to Emergency, someone said the hospital was bursting at the seams, that there were no beds at all. He could feel the frenzy and the noise past reception.

You can turn people around, his registrar had scolded him. You're here to keep them alive, you know.

Is he? Why is he? Why is that the most important thing? Bodies with circulation and breath but, so often, hardly life. Ambulances arriving endlessly, wailing their urgency to restock the building's store of bodies.

They'd gone to her room after leaving Dr Chester with the team, drunk wine and stood at the window sharing the cigarette Mary Doyle had given him a whole lifetime ago. The room looked out over the back of the hospital and their faces were lit in the ambulance strobes that came and went. Like they were watching a firework display.

Maybe it's the same ambulance going round and round, he said to her. All the melodrama of saving life but never valuing it.

We could buy our own ambulance, she said. Hurtle out to missed moments with the sirens blaring. Then she said, Here's an unmissed moment. And kissed him.

Lying down, still dressed, they'd fallen instantly and deeply asleep.

He's sat on this bus so many times with Ben or others, like being on a school bus, both grateful and hurt by the company. Ben sits sounding off about patients, like they're press-ups at the gym. People can hear him but he doesn't care. No, it isn't that. He just doesn't feel it, doesn't feel the ache of their hearing. But you can't make other people feel things or ache, he sees that now.

What would Ben say, seeing him now on the bus with her? Maybe he'd insist on explaining what sleeping with someone actually fucking means, Sebastian. That you have to take your fucking clothes off, mate.

But he's through with it all now, their version of events – Ben's, his registrar's, the lot of them – all of medicine's repeating follies.

They look out together at crowds hurrying through the rain, sheltering under doorways, the night filled surprisingly with life. She pulls his hand and they stand together, walk over to the front of the bus and ask to be let out. The doors swing open and the road multiplies light, pillars of it like a world on bright stilts, or one set adrift and trailing ribbons.

We can race matchsticks, she says. Or find the deer. Be careless anyway.

They step down from the bus, out in between hospitals and into the rain.

Dev Bhatia, consultant physician and James Chester, consultant oncologist

Sunday, 30 October

HOW FAR DO YOU want to go?

With you? Jim says. All the way, surely?

Easily tipped over these wheelchairs. Often tragically.
No one would care. And you'd just feel bad about it.

Let's stop here for a bit.

Your bench? Blimey, Dr Bhatia, I'm honoured.

It isn't mine. Behave.

Might as well be, look. Dev-shaped arse hollowed into the wood.

Identifiably pert?

Identifiably troubled, I'd say. And a little flabby.

*

He sits here sometimes after work. The bench faces over to Outpatients, its doors opening and closing like heart valves. The hills rise over it, burnished now in the late, stray light.

People used to stop and talk to him as they left the building, but less so these days, just the occasional nod from a new doctor. Like so much else, the consistency of the thing renders it invisible.

He remembers leaving a late shift once as a junior in London and actually stepping over a patient. The man lay belly-up between the two sets of sliding doors in Emergency, unkempt and drunk. Someone he'd clerked in many times, a regular. It was a big step to cross the man's substantial girth. Almost a leap, really. Up and over him, then clean out of the exit. Purposeful but unconscious.

It wasn't until he arrived in Soho later, and was drinking with friends, that he realised what he'd done and felt it for the first time. How some things, important things, become pedestrian just through their repetition in medicine.

How'd I ever miss this view, Jim says.

Busy people. You'll know to look at it now, I guess.

After my hospital epiphanies, on the receiving end of you doctors?

Yeah, well. I've always thought it's the doctors that are receiving something.

Bingo. All of medicine in a sentence.

Hopefully you'll be home soon?

Oh please, not more hope.

Fine.

You look like shit, Dev.

Says a sick old man.

Yeah well, you can't kid a kidder.

I'm OK, just tired.

The moment of the kiss repeats. The shock of it, her skin. A patient. For that moment, his patient.

She had the scan on Friday. He'll look at it tomorrow with one of the radiologists, her fortune, then release her out to it, like a paper boat to water.

He remembers, as a medical student, one of the registrars saying something that's stuck with him. Hailed as one of the brightest things around, winning medals and the consultants' clear admiration, she was completely effortless and cool in her passage through medicine. That day, she was presenting someone's history to them on the ward round.

A fascinating case, she said, slotting the X-ray up to the light box and demonstrating the filigree lines of the man's pneumonitis. Then, almost as a casual aside, she said, He's had a good life, he's got no regrets. Odd, in hindsight, that she should say it at all. Perhaps it was just an extravagance, like a bow tie on a would-be professor.

But he took it as a statement of fact then, like the true course of the facial nerve or the correct dose of amoxycillin. That the unwell man lacked regrets. That this skilled and intelligent doctor was capable of discerning it. And that an absence of regret was a central criterion of a good life, a life well lived.

Ah, look. The moon's up over Chester car park.

With a Chester-shaped dent in the tarmac.

When the moon's white like that you really see it, don't you? For what it is.

A ball of rock?

Yep. Pummelled rock. Not some pretty night light.

Last of the romantics, you.

Let's get all those doctors out and show it to them.

What for?

A bit of awe. Set the fire alarms off, Dev. Get them bloody out here.

*

A woman arrives by the doors, dressing gown open and lifting in the breeze, her white nightie visible. That lady from the other morning who asked if he was frightened, holding on to her drip stand like she's at the helm of a ship. She ignores all the signs and lights up a cigarette. Astonishing, her recovery.

Some recoveries are so hard to fathom. Not just individual patients but the whole building, always renewing itself. He's walked away from tragic scenes and moments and then, crossing this space on the way to radiology or intensive care, found himself by couples leaving maternity, carrying out new, wailing life. All of it happening in parallel.

He might have said all this to her. He can imagine her laughing at him but knows he could have said it. He feels the kiss again, the punch of intimacy, blinks it away.

I followed this guy in the other day, Jim says. I'd not long told him and his wife some scan results and they were in pieces, you know. He must've gone to sort his parking out or something because ten minutes later I'm behind him again at those doors.

And?

And he looked so ordinary.

Ordinary?

He looked fine. Completely fine.

Like you wouldn't know what had happened?

Thing is, though, you look around and . . .

I know. Other people's lives.

I was in Paddington with Emily the next morning and fuck, Dev, all those people.

Their stories?

Who'd know?

Come on, let's get you in. The nurses will be pining.

Take me outside for a bit?

Out there?

Bars and restaurants are warming up, even on a Sunday evening, surprisingly. Like an orchestra tuning. The sky's still bright, low down between roofs. He wheels Jim over the uneven paving, struggling with the effort of it, sweating a little.

They pass a pub with a crowd outside, someone singing. Lucy and one of the porters sit with others at a table. A drunken cheer rises as someone notices them and calls out. Dr Chester, they shout, Dr Bat-yer, come and have a beer. Come give us a kiss.

THANK YOU

Ian Nesbitt, for kindly allowing me to use his *A Lie Softly Spoken* (BMJ 2002;324:1122) for Lucy's story

Rose Tomaszewska, Fiona Carpenter, Elizabeth Masters & everyone at riverrun

Everyone at Janklow & Nesbit

Agnes Davis, Alice Jolly, Cas Harte, Charlie Candish, Christopher Potter, Claire Morgan, Daisy Johnson, Diana Patient, Elaine Todman, Gabriel Weston, Iona Heath, Jane Draycott, Janette Corrick, Jenny Valentine, Joanna Palmer, John Carey, John Ninian, Jo Shapcott, Kate Turner, Kiran Millwood Hargrave, Lionel Shriver, Maria Slattery, Mark Read, Marti Leimbach, Peter Thomas, Ray Tallis, Rhidian Brook, Rory Gleeson, Sacha Vitarana, Sarvat Hassin, Sean Elyan, Shahla Haque, Sushma Guglani, Tom de Freston, Tom Roques, Unruly Writers & Vicky Bell

Claire Conrad & Jon Riley

K.A.

Joseph, Eve & Alison, for the surprise

Sudarshan Kumar Guglani, for telling me stories

A NOTE ON THE TYPE

In 1924, Monotype based this face on types cut by
Pierre Simon Fournier c. 1742. These types were some
of the most influential designs of the eighteenth century,
being among the earliest of the transitional style of
typeface, and were a stepping stone to the more severe
modern style made popular by Bodoni later in the
century. They had more vertical stress than the old style
types, greater contrast between thick and thin strokes and
little or no bracketing on the serifs.